The Savior of 6th Street

The Savior of 6th Street

ORLANDO ORTEGA-MEDINA

Cloud Lodge Books

London

First published in the United Kingdom in 2020
by Cloud Lodge Books (CLB)

A CIP catalogue record for this book is available from the British Library.

ISBN 978-1-8380451-0-4

1 3 5 7 9 10 8 6 4 2

Cover Art © Gerardo Castro
Afrofuturism Yemaya, 2015, diptych, oil on wood, mixed media
www.GerardoCastroArt.com

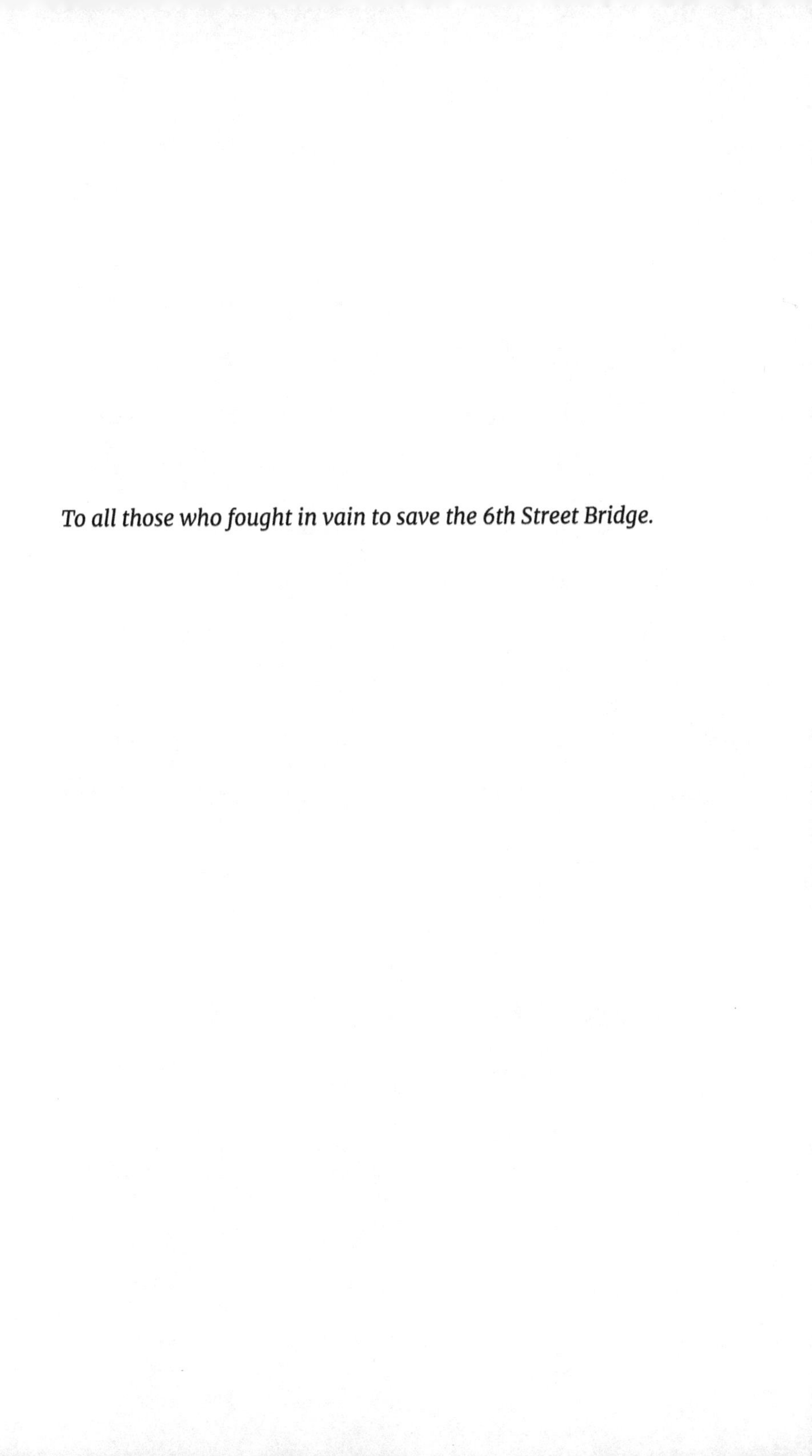

To all those who fought in vain to save the 6th Street Bridge.

Contents

1

Savior

I read in the papers that Beatrice Schein died last week in a fireball. The small biplane she was traveling in fell out of the sky and came crashing down over the Kalahari, scattering the confetti of human remains across ten miles of searing desert. The first thing I thought was she would have loved reading that obituary; she'd always craved a romantic death.

Then came the tears.

For one year Beatrice had been my Lucifer, my star of the morning. She'd entered my world as if descending from Heaven intent on pulling me out of Hades. She didn't realize until it was too late that I am as much a part of this place as the rotting buildings that are cemented into these mad streets. Removal requires demolition. Besides, I like it here.

My name is Virgilio Santos — Saint Virgil to my friends — former street artist and small-time savior. I live in a tenement with my dear mother and mentor Celia the Divine at the edge of Downtown Los Angeles at the corner of 6th and Alameda — a couple of blocks from the vast 6th Street Viaduct where a magnificent double-arched talking bridge spans the trickle-torrent that is the Los Angeles River. Just beyond our tenement lies grime-choked Skid Row and beyond that the sparkling towers of Downtown LA.

I had just turned twenty in 1988, the summer Beatrice spotted me a little over two years ago. She was twenty-seven then. She and her friend Anne wandered into the community arts center, where I spent most of my evenings painting *aché*-infused tableaus inspired by my blessed life.

'Get a load of those two,' Sexto, the center assistant, said, jerking his thumb in their direction. He was only sixteen and still had the wiry body of an adolescent. But already he oozed sexuality and was forever seeking any opportunity to, as he put it, stick it somewhere.

I looked down from the top of the ladder, where I was busy hanging the last of my paintings for our annual art show, and spotted Beatrice and Anne strolling around the warehouse that served as the center's exhibition space. Although they were both dressed in jeans and T-shirts, I could tell they weren't from the neighborhood. Beatrice was the most conspicuous of the two, with her Boho style shoulder-length auburn hair, her lithe ballet dancer's body, and the way she seemed to glide when she walked, her head held up as if she were sniffing rarefied air. Anne was a tall, big-chested woman in her thirties who sported a pair of sapphire blue cat-eye glasses. She wore her chestnut brown hair pinned up in the back and smiled a lot.

Sexto winked at me, hiked up his chinos, and Gumbied across the floor to them, and I turned to finish my work. When I climbed down a few minutes later, I found the three of them at the foot of the ladder staring up at my painting. Anne had removed her glasses and was screwing up her eyes at it; Beatrice was standing a little to one side, her mouth slightly open, her eyes wide.

'This is Saint Virgil.' Sexto bowed to me with an exaggerated flourish. 'He's the artist. Those are his too.' He lifted his head at four other paintings to the right of the ladder. But the women continued to stare at the one I'd just hung, the largest of the lot.

Anne stepped up to the title card mounted on the wall and scanned the media details, then she turned and stared at the painting again.

'It's magnificent,' Beatrice said, looking at me. 'What do you call it?'

Anne jumped in as I opened my mouth, 'It's called *The Savior of 6th Street*.' She nodded at the title card.

'It's his self-portrait,' Sexto added, beaming a gap-toothed smile.

I'd worked on the painting for six weeks. It contained within it all the elements of my life, the tenement block where I live, the rush hour traffic that grinds past our building at the end of each working day when the city workers abandon the downtown to those of us who live there. And floating high above, gazing down on it all, was me, naked as the day I was expelled from God's womb, my arms extended, a crown of nails encircling my head, a sacred heart blazing from my chest, hot to the touch of any who dared get that close to it.

Anne stepped back and removed her glasses. 'It's an intriguing title.'

'It's an intriguing *painting*.' Beatrice stepped up to it. 'Very striking.'

'Thank you,' I said.

'He really does have a tattoo on his chest like that one.' Sexto flashed a sly smile and tugged at my T-shirt. I squeezed his shoulder affectionately and moved his arm away.

'The contrasting Christ image is quite beautiful set against that bleak background,' Beatrice said. 'It suffuses the scene with a profound sense of hope.' She turned and locked eyes with me. They were lovely eyes, a light shade of violet ringed with dark brown. I'd never seen anything like them.

'Did you actually use yourself as a model?' she asked, her face expressionless as a Byzantine Madonna.

'He does martial arts and gymnastics.' Sexto pumped his eyebrows and looked back and forth between the women. 'He's totally ripped like that. I've seen him with his shirt off.'

Beatrice nodded. Her eyes wandered, lingering at my sternum a bit too long for my comfort.

'It's not just a self-portrait,' I said. 'It's meant to represent the daytime world I inhabit, which I wouldn't necessarily call bleak.' I climbed the ladder again and, using a ruler as a pointer, spent the next few minutes interpreting the painting to the women, who listened quietly. When I finished, Beatrice exchanged a glance with Anne.

'Is there a companion piece — for your nighttime world?' Anne asked.

Sexto broke into a nervous snigger and turned away.

I touched the ruler to my forehead. 'It's in here, mostly.'

I climbed down the ladder and folded it closed. 'Sorry, ladies, but we have to finish setting up. If you want to poke around some more make sure you get permission from the director.' I pointed at a door at the back of the exhibition space. 'Her office is over there.'

'Very kind, thank you,' Beatrice said lightly. 'But I think we'll be going.'

Anne nodded and glanced at the scores of other paintings ranged around the room, some on the floor leaning against the wall, others already mounted. Sexto sidled up to us with a wide grin and took a last opportunity to discreetly size up the two women.

'One final question before we go, if I may,' Beatrice said.

I shrugged. 'Sure, why not.'

'Why the self-indulgent savior image — you exalted over the city like that? You didn't explain that.'

I pointed at the painting again. 'The figure is sacrificed, not exalted. There's a universe of difference between those two doctrines.'

'Fair enough,' she said, 'But what are you meant to be saving?'

'Everything,' I said, 'Whatever needs fixing.'

'I see,' Beatrice said, trying her best to suppress a smile. 'You're the local Superman.'

'Something like that.' I handed the ruler to Sexto and wiped my hands on my jeans. 'I'm afraid we're out of time, ladies. It's been a pleasure.'

'Those two were smokin'!' Sexto said after they'd left. He flashed a smile and ran his hand over his shaved head.

'They were all right.' I picked up my supplies and moved to the storage room to pack them away, still reflecting on Beatrice's eyes.

'What do you suppose they were doing here?'

I shrugged. 'You should've asked them.'

'I did! They said they read about the center in a magazine and were curious to see it.'

'There you go.'

* * *

The show opened on Saturday evening. It was a gala event meant to raise funds for the center. We'd invited a lot of influential people from the arts community, including collectors, critics, and potential benefactors. The mayor was there, and some of the city council members showed up as well.

My date for the night was Concha Morales, my best friend and confidante, who in high school was known as Jesús, la Dominicana. I wore a pair of tan linen trousers, a crisp white *guayabera* my mother ordered special from Miami, and dark brown penny loafers; Concha wore a blue-and-white kimono she had found on sale in a shop in J-Town that complemented her ebony skin. She'd pinned up her hair and held it in place with a pair of black ceramic chopsticks, like a Caribbean geisha.

We were standing next to the drinks table knocking back margaritas and exchanging words with some of the other artists when I spotted Beatrice and Anne navigating the crowd on their way to where we were standing. Beatrice had completely transformed herself. Off-white strapless evening gown, curled hair cascading out of a blue pillbox hat, and a pair of pearl earrings set in white gold. Anne looked particularly splendid in a little black dress and heels. Gone were the cat-eye glasses. She looked like a young and edible Jacqueline Kennedy.

'Those are the ones I told you about,' I said to Concha out of the side of my mouth. She grabbed hold of my arm as Beatrice and Anne broke free of the crowd and stepped up to us.

'Well, look who's here,' I said, extending my hand to Anne. Beatrice intercepted it midair.

'I'm sorry we didn't properly introduce ourselves the other day,' she said. 'I'm Beatrice Schein, and this is Anne Levine. Anne writes for the *Herald Examiner*.'

I smiled and shook her hand, then nodded at Concha.

'This is my friend Concha.'

'What a wonderful event,' Anne said, looking around the room.

Beatrice continued to stare at me, her lovely eyes shining in the bright lights. I found myself mentally calculating which combination of oils I would use to approximate their complex color on canvas. Concha nudged my leg with her knee.

'I'm Virgilio, by the way.'

'Not Saint Virgil?' Beatrice said with an unmistakable hint of irony.

'Virgilio Santos, actually. Some of my friends call me Saint Virgil just for fun. Anyway, what's your story?'

Beatrice pulled back her hand and frowned a little. 'I'm the curator of a private art collection. I'm also a collector in my own right. I was curious about this show.'

I turned and snatched a couple of glasses of white wine off the serving table and handed them to Beatrice and Anne.

'Well, in that case, welcome to East Side Arts and Graphics,' I said with a smile.

Beatrice quickly recovered herself and nodded before taking a sip of wine. A slight grimace registered on her flawless face as the wine hit her tongue.

'A lot of fine artists are exhibiting here tonight,' I continued.

I waved over Lucinda Arechaederra, the director of the center, and introduced her to Beatrice and Anne. She took over from there and shepherded them toward the exhibit. As they moved away, Beatrice tossed a lingering glance over her shoulder at me before continuing.

'What a total bitch,' Concha said once they'd gone. She grabbed another margarita and downed it in one gulp.

'What do you mean?' I took the glass out of her hand and pressed a bottle of mineral water into it. 'She seemed okay to me.'

'You mean she wanted to eat you for dessert like you were a cream-filled chocolate éclair. She downright ignored me, the stuck-up bimbo. Her friend too.'

'Whoa there. What's got your panties in a twist?'

She reached for another margarita, and I pulled back her hand.

'I hate those rich bitches. Everyone's beneath them.'

'Come on, *preciosa*,' I said, pulling her along by the arm. 'Let's get you some fresh air.'

I took her outside to the courtyard patio and sat with her on a bench. She looked up at the sky, which was free of clouds and starless. Her dark eyes were brimming with tears threatening to overflow and streak her makeup. I reached into my pocket, pulled out a black bandana, and dabbed them dry. Concha wrapped her arms around me and rested her head on my shoulder. We stayed that way for a while, then she straightened up and looked down at the concrete.

'What is it?' I asked.

'One of these days someone's going to whisk you away from here. You know that, don't you?'

'Don't say that, Concha.' I kissed her forehead.

'It's true. You're too good for all this. And that bitch knows it.' She jabbed a blue-lacquered fingernail at the center. 'She'll take you away from me.'

'I'm not going anywhere.'

'You'd better not, *pendejo*. I don't know what I'd do if I ever lost you.'

I stood and stretched my legs. 'Enough with the dramatics. Let's go back inside. I don't want to be rude.'

'You go, *mijo*. I'll look for you later. I need to be alone for a bit.' She kissed my hand and waved me away.

I went back inside and pressed my way through the crowd. I couldn't see how they'd be able to fit anyone else into the place. I bounced on my toes to look over the heads and saw a pair of minders holding back a mass of people at the door.

'Did you see them?' I heard someone say. I turned and saw Sexto in a too-tight tuxedo sucking on a bottle of sparkling water. 'Those *fresas* from the other day. Turns out they're big wheelers.'

'I saw them.'

'One of them has a hard-on for your work. The prettier one.'

I spotted Concha slipping into the room. I waved at her and pointed at the side exit. She nodded and moved toward it.

'I'm going to cut out, man,' I said. 'It's getting crazy in here. I can barely breathe.'

Sexto took hold of my arm. 'Hey, *vato*, before you go...'

'Yeah?'

'Come to dinner on Saturday at my *abuelita*'s. It's her eightieth birthday. I'm making tamales.' A wide grin broke out on his face. 'Best ones in the city, guaranteed.'

'Sure, I'll come.' I gave him a quick hug. 'But I've got to run now, sorry.'

'No problem. Just make sure to wear a rubber with that one.' Sexto winked at me and disappeared into the crowd.

I pushed my way to the side exit through the press of people and had almost caught up with Concha when one of the other artists grabbed me by the arm.

'Hey, Santos, congratulations.'

I looked around at him and lifted my head questioningly.

'Haven't you heard?' he shouted over the music, which had suddenly increased in volume. 'Some rich chick just bought your paintings. Every single one.'

I glanced at Concha, who flashed a sad smile and slipped out the side exit. I gave a thumbs-up to my artist friend and squeezed the rest of the way through the crowd toward the door. When I finally made it out of the building, I looked up and down the empty streets, but Concha had vanished into the night.

2

Yemaya

The door to my apartment flew open the moment my fingers touched the doorknob, and I unexpectedly found myself facing my mother across our cramped living room illuminated only by the flickering votive candles on our family altar: Celia the Divine, *Madre del Todo*, my mentor and protector, black as a vein of onyx, her sky blue eyes wide and all-seeing. She was dressed in the mustard and white gingham uniform of the all-night diner where she worked, her heavily salted kinky black hair pinned into a bun and topped off by a matching waitress cap.

'Come inside, *hijo*,' she said, beckoning me forward. She was gripping a cigar in her hand, a trail of smoke ascending to the ceiling from its glowing end.

'What are you still doing home, Mamá?' I crossed the threshold and set down my backpack.

'I've been waiting for you.' She kissed my forehead and pointed her cigar at the altar. 'Face *Changó*.'

'Not now, Mamá.'

'Yes, now.' She jabbed her cigar again at the altar.

Discreetly rolling my eyes, I faced the multilevel altar on the top of which she had arranged a trinity of *orishas* impersonating Catholic saints: leprous San Lazaro followed by three mangy street dogs, lapping at his oozing sores; the glorious Virgen del Cobre, ascending like Godzilla out of a storm-churned Caribbean over three tiny men in a dinghy; and positioned between them, presiding over the pantheon, stood awesome Santa Barbara, properly known as Changó, majestic in her flowing blue cape, blood-red gown, and golden crown, her skin as black as a moonless night.

An ornate, hand-painted wood-framed mirror hanging on the wall above the altar allowed me to make eye contact with Celia as she put the fat cigar to her lips and drew a long draught of smoke into her lungs, her large chest slowly puffing up. After what seemed an eternity, she exhaled over me, emptying her lungs of the protective smoke she'd been incubating inside. Drawing in another chestful, she held it for several seconds, blew another long stream of smoke over the length of my body, and chanted an incantation in *Lucumí*.

I glanced over my shoulder at her. 'What's this about, Mamá?'

'Breathe in,' she said.

'But—'

She poked at the air with her cigar. 'Face Changó and breathe in.'

Knowing better than to argue with her when she was in *Santera* queen mode, I shook my head and complied. Celia narrowed her eyes and studied me in the mirror, then she lunged forward and spun me around. Bringing her head close to mine, she pressed her index finger to the area between my eyebrows, and a warm current streamed into my face. I resisted the urge to pull away and calmed myself by slowing down my breathing. Celia's face relaxed as she matched the rise and fall of my chest, and a sense of calm descended over the room.

'I did well tonight, Mamá,' I ventured after a few moments of silence, hoping the ritual had come to an end.

'Hush!' She drew back her finger, opened her hand, and held it over my head. A static charge caused my hair to levitate toward her open palm. Then her eyes widened as the room turned black and filled with the sound of flapping wings approaching.

When I regained consciousness, I found myself slumped over our retro dining table across from my mother who was leaning back in her chair, its two front legs lifted off the floor, her head cocked to one side. Staring at me. Waiting. Her eyes growing wider. A painful weariness in my limbs, as if I'd just completed an intense workout at the gym, told me she'd summoned an extra-potent dose of aché into my body. I pivoted my head to glance at the wall clock and saw it was nearly eleven o'clock, a full hour since I'd arrived home. Apparently, I'd lost thirty minutes of my life to the process.

'What's happening, Mamá?' I struggled to get to my feet, then gave up and dropped back into my chair.

She rocked forward and slid a demitasse of steaming Cuban coffee across the table that seemed to have materialized from out of nowhere. I pulled it to myself and negotiated a mouthful of the searingly hot, bittersweet syrup, then set the little cup back on its saucer and pushed it aside with a sweep of my hand.

'You needed extra protection, mijo.'

'I'm fine, Mamá. There's no need to worry. Everything's going really well. I sold all my paintings tonight.'

'I'm aware.' She cradled my hands in hers. 'And I'm extremely proud of you.' She squeezed my hands tight. 'But be very careful, mijo. There's danger in success, and in this success in particular.'

I pulled back my hands and sat up.

'*Oshún* showed me,' she said, invoking the name of my protector. 'She showed *her* to me.'

'She showed who to you?'

'The woman who bought your work.' She closed her eyes and chanted under her breath. When she opened them again only the whites were showing. 'There's darkness behind it all,' she said. 'That's why I summoned you home.'

'I came of my own volition, Mamá.'

She let out a chuckle and rose to her full height, her eyes normal again. 'Nothing is of our own volition, mijo. You should know that by now.'

I gave a little shrug and nodded, acknowledging the lesson she'd drilled into me ever since I was old enough to understand anything. She'd pressed it home all the harder after my father walked out on us when I was just four years old, which had left me bereft with a massive wound in my heart that took aeons to clot and scar over.

She retrieved her coat and purse from the closet and readied herself to go. 'Anyway, now that I've sealed you, I can rest more easily.'

I followed her to the front door and gave her a kiss on the cheek.

'But be extra careful, mijo. And stay home tonight, please. None of your prowling about.'

'I can't, Mamá. I've got to go find Concha. She was upset.'

My mother shook her head. 'Be careful with that one too.'

'Yes, yes, I'll be careful. Now, shoo! You're already late for work. I'll see you in the morning.'

She gazed at me one last time before vanishing into the dimly lit hallway of our tenement. After a moment, I pushed the door closed and drew a deep breath. The aromatic smell of cigar smoke lingering in the room made me reflect on her warnings. Her overprotective nature colored her judgement when it came to me, and over the years she'd often subjected me to maddening bouts of senseless anxiety and panic. But there was no denying she was a gifted Santera with a highly developed spiritual faculty. So, I thought, maybe it was best to take heed and watch my back for the next few days, just in case.

Stepping into my bedroom, I changed into a pair of well-worn 501s, a black T-shirt, and black and white checkered Vans; then I climbed out my window onto the fire escape, slid down to the sidewalk, and sprinted through the wretched darkness of Skid Row on my way downtown.

3

La Magdalena

I cut through a dark, junk-strewn alley on my way to Broadway, and sped past monstrous green garbage bins overflowing with the unnamable; discarded mattresses stained with bodily fluids; carcasses of television sets; shredded truck tires; dented oil barrels flickering in the night; charity bags replete with hand-me-downs; Swiss cheese shoes; the rotting corpses of pets now unrecognizable. As I neared the middle of the alley, I noted movement in the shadows. Someone was shooting up junk there; another someone was pissing in a corner over there. A rat scuttled past my feet as I picked up the pace.

Just before I exited onto Broadway, I spotted a large bearded man — forty or fiftysomething — clad crown to heel in black leather and smoking a thick cigar, standing next to a rusted air conditioning unit, his back arched, his head thrown back. On the ground in front of him was someone, male or female I couldn't tell, on their knees and lapping at his boots. Both of them paused for an instant and glanced at me as I passed them. Leather Man flicked his cigar at me; it sputtered and sparked across the asphalt until it came to rest on the other side of the alley. Perfect. I burned the image into the right side of my brain, saving it for later, and dashed out of the alley.

I sprinted past the darkened buildings and abandoned picture palaces, dodging an army of streeters pushing shopping carts along the sidewalk filled with the flotsam of their lives. A few blocks later, I turned onto 3rd Street and dipped into a crowded dive bar with loud, distorted Latin pop music blaring out of a pair of cracked speakers. This was the incongruously named La Noche Buena cabaret. The place reeked of beer and Lysol, its trademark scent, as iconic as Chanel No. 5.

At the far end of the stifling room was a backdrop of Rio de Janeiro of all places — an aerial view of the city photographed from behind the colossal Christ the Redeemer statue. The image of Rio overlooked a small stage on which a busty Mexican transvestite in pink satin hot pants was twerking and lip-synching to an Ana Gabriel song. Concha was standing to one side of the stage below the DJ box, waiting for her turn to come on. She was stunning in a green satin evening gown, black velvet choker, and reddish-brown Veronica Lake wig. Mesmerized by the performance on stage, she lip-synched along with the song.

I scored a beer at the bar and worked my way toward Concha just as she ascended the stage and stood in front of the microphone, which was now live. Concha surveyed her audience from under the long lashes that graced her emerald green eyes. The crowd grew quiet waiting for the music to start. She smiled at them and glanced at the DJ, catching my eye as she did so. I lifted my hand as the music came on. She responded by sticking out her tongue at me before turning back to the microphone and grinding out a sultry rendition of *Somewhere Over the Rainbow* in her bittersweet, smooth-as-a chocolate-shake voice. She worked the room like a pro, moving through the crowd as it parted for her, collecting dollar bills and telephone numbers, which she stuffed into her cleavage. Then she reascended the little stage to perform a second number at the insistence of her admirers.

I greeted her with a hug when she descended from the stage to the din of mad applause. She responded by pulling me into the small, dimly lit dressing room next to the toilets and planting a lingering kiss on my lips. I looked into her eyes, and she shook her head, placing two fingers on my mouth.

'Don't,' she said. 'Let me pretend for a bit.'

'Pretend what?'

'That you love me.'

'I do love you.'

'You know what I mean, pendejo.'

I rolled my eyes and took a sip from my beer. Concha snatched the bottle out of my hand and guzzled the rest, then she tossed it at an overflowing plastic trashcan, missing it by six inches. The bottle clattered to the floor and rolled into a corner.

'Nice one.'

Concha shrugged and leaned in toward me.

'Why did you run out on me at the exhibition?' I asked, moving my head away from her.

She grabbed the back of my neck and kissed me again, this time more passionately, and I let her, which I knew was something of a calculated risk. After a moment, Concha came up for air and turned to lock the door.

'No, Concha.'

'Why not?'

'You know why not.'

A loud pounding startled us. Concha pulled open the door and hissed a few choice words at one of the other performers, then slammed it shut and stared at me.

'I can give it up, you know,' she said after a moment. 'I do it more for the company than the money.'

'Whatever. Why did you run out on me?'

'Because, Loverboy, I didn't belong there.'

'Don't call me that, please.'

'I'm sorry. I just wish it were true, that's all.

'We've been over this countless times,' I said. 'You're my best friend, and aside from my mother, the only woman in my life.'

'I want more.'

'There's nothing more.'

'What about the future? Don't you want someone for yourself? Someone to share your life with, to make a home with?'

'Frankly, no.'

'I don't believe you.' Concha kicked the trashcan, knocking it over and sending empty beer bottles rolling across the floor.

'Even if I did, it wouldn't be you.'

'Ouch.'

'I'm not telling you anything you don't already know.'

'I'm sure if the right opportunity came around, you'd jump at it.'

'What do you mean, the right opportunity?'

'It's a figure of speech, babe.'

'Maybe it is; maybe it isn't. But I don't appreciate it.' I moved toward the door and Concha grabbed hold of my arm.

'Don't go, please,' she said. 'I'm sorry. I was just caught a bit off guard by that rich chick buying all your paintings. It felt like the beginning of the end for us.'

'I hate to break it to you, Concha, but artists who don't sell their paintings starve. Her buying my paintings is a *good* thing. You should be happy for me, not throwing a tantrum.'

Concha lowered her gaze and stared at the floor for a bit, then drew a deep breath and nodded absently. The volume of the pounding dance music outside increased, making the door vibrate. After a moment, Concha looked me straight in the eye. Something in them had gone suddenly dead.

'I'm going,' she said, turning to leave.

'Concha, wait.'

Later she mouthed, drying her eyes before withdrawing and leaving me alone.

I dropped back onto the chair to collect my thoughts just as a group of drag queens burst into the room to change out of their costumes. I watched them for a bit, trying my best to compose a new tableau in my head if only to clear my mind. But my conversation with Concha kept coming back, and I found myself worrying I may have been too harsh with her. So I slipped out of the dressing room to find her.

It was already 1:30 in the morning, and the crowd had thinned out quite a lot. I cast about the room searching for Concha and caught sight of her at the back conversing intimately with a grey-haired man in a pinstripe suit, no tie, open shirt, who had his hand on her ass. She raised her head as I approached and lifted a finger at me, just enough for me to catch her message. I shrugged and walked out the door. She knew where to find me if she needed me.

As I walked home from the bar, the hum of drills and the glow of tungsten lights over by Alameda Street caught my attention, and I opted instead to see how things were going with the construction of the new subway line.

4

Gehenna

Los Angeles needed an underground train, a subway system. At least that's what they told us. (Whoever they were.) I didn't pay much attention to politics in those days. I still don't. They tried to ram it down our throats for years, got initiatives balloted and rejected by the voters more than a few times. Finally, one day, somehow, the measure passed, and the MTA was born. Construction workers descended on downtown one night in the late 1980s after the office workers had left and started tunneling under the streets.

They worked section-by-section, digging, removing debris, reinforcing, securing, and moving on to the next section. Others would come later, depending on funding, and wire it up, lay tracks, and, eventually, kit out the stations. They were building a station a block from where I lived. Nobody was sure when it was going to be finished. There were rumors of five years, ten years, never. In the meantime, we who lived there had to endure the noise and dust and blinding white lights they turned on once the twilight had burned itself out and didn't turn off until the first glimmer of dawn.

I made my way to Alameda Street, toward the rumbling of the digging machines. When I reached the corner opposite the construction area,

I had to shield my eyes with my hand against the harsh light of the tungsten lamps that illuminated the site and the area under the street. Imagine those gigantic rotating spotlights they used back in the day to shoot shafts of light into the sky to promote movie premiers and county fairs, only beamed into your face instead of the sky. That.

The workers had set up enormous plastic tarps over the construction area to limit the amount of dust, and God-knows-what-else that got kicked up into the atmosphere as a result of their drilling. I could see the workers through the plastic moving in and out of the access breach they had built to give them ingress to the digging area under the street. They wore what looked like space suits and helmets.

Most of my neighbors hated the whole thing. The all-night noise made it difficult to sleep, and those of us who lived close to the digging sites found it challenging to block out the glare from those tungsten lamps, short of painting our windows black. But I loved it. The chaos, the noise, the bright lights, the spacemen — the not-very-secure tunnels they left in their wake where a whole other plane of existence unfolded each night.

I wandered along the sidewalk to where the construction site ended and crossed to the other side of the street then walked south a couple of blocks to one of the tunnel access points. There were several of them along the path where the line would one day be installed. The workers had closed them off. But people found their way into the tunnels anyhow. At first, the security folk and the cops tried chasing them out. But the moment they cleared one area, the tunnel people found their way into another. Chasing people out of tunnels was too expensive and wasn't planned for in the budget. So at the end of the day, the contractor gave up and abandoned the tunnels to the tunnel people, knowing the problem would be taken care of once the area was wired up and the tracks installed, and they were forced back into the sewers, abandoned factories, empty warehouses, and back alleys from which they'd come.

I slid past a partially open, rusted iron door that wouldn't close anymore and put up my hand just as the flashlight I expected shone in my face. The black guy standing guard snapped it off as soon as he recognized me and gave me a high five. As I walked past him to the access ladder, he tapped me on the shoulder and asked for a cigarette, lifting his head and putting two fingers to his lips, the way he did every time he saw me. I shrugged and shook my head. He laughed and dropped back into his chair. It was a ritual I didn't understand. But it worked.

I slid down the access ladder, dropped onto the concrete floor, and looked up and down the curve of the empty central tunnel, which echoed with a hodgepodge of sounds floating at me from various quarters, live rancheras, recorded arias, suppressed laughter, the unmistakable moans of pleasure and pain, and punctuating it all from time to time, raucous cheers that erupted out of one of the side tunnels near me. In the distance, I could make out the blur of people crossing between side tunnels, each of which contained its own unique little world.

Flames flickering in disused oil barrels illuminated the central tunnel. There was one barrel set up every twenty-five yards or so all the way along as far as one could see. They were maintained by a wiry Chinese boy dressed in a clean black jumpsuit who looked to be about thirteen-years-old. Everyone called him Bruce Lee. I asked him once where his parents were and who was paying him. But he didn't seem to speak or understand English. Nobody else I asked knew anything about him. We just accepted he was included in the price of admission and left it at that. I did sketch him once and gave him a tenner for posing for me. He'd made it into one of the paintings from the exhibition that Beatrice had purchased, a portrait of a cocky Chinese boy in black standing next to a flickering oil barrel set against a black background out of which stared a dozen malevolent mismatched eyes. I called it *Neglect*.

As I moved south, Bruce Lee popped out of one of the side tunnels, his arms laden with newsprint, and ran in my direction, inspecting each of the barrels and feeding the flames. I reached out and tousled his oily hair as he passed, eliciting a playful scream from him. I wiped my hand on my jeans as I turned and watched him recede into the distance.

A few other men dropped into the tunnel. Dark trousers, dinner jackets, no tie. They glanced in my direction as they moved past, murmuring among themselves as if seeing through me. I recognized one of them from a couple of nights ago, a cherub-faced red-haired thirtysomething with a late case of acne who lagged behind the others. I nodded at him, but he didn't acknowledge my greeting. Instead, he looked away, picked up his pace and followed the others into the side tunnel where the cheering was coming from. I jogged behind them and ducked into it, emerging into a concrete chamber crammed with men of all races and ages, dressed in everything from tuxedos to blue jeans. They were ranged in a semicircle along the walls. The smoke-filled air was rank with the stink of cigars, cigarettes, alcohol, perspiration, and blood.

Into the middle of the crowd, on a space cleared on the floor, strode a desiccated old man from the back of the chamber. Sweaty T-shirt, dirty chinos, flip flops, a hat made of dry palm leaves, a cigar clenched between his toothless gums. In one hand he carried a live rooster up-sidedown by its legs. The red-hooded animal squawked and desperately flapped its wings. The crowd erupted into loud cheers as the old man held up the rooster and spun on his feet to display it to everyone.

A moment later a tall, muscular boy of around seventeen or eighteen walked into the middle space from out of the background, shirtless and carrying a struggling blue-hooded rooster by the legs. He was fiercely handsome; his skin burnished a dark red by the sun, his shoulder-length black hair glistening in the firelight. When he reached the middle of the chamber, he raised the struggling rooster over his head and regarded the screaming crowd with narrowed eyes, his head held up, baring his teeth at them. He turned around slowly making sure everyone in the chamber got a good look at his rooster. He made brief eye contact with me as I pulled a sketchpad out of my backpack and leaned against the wall, readying myself to capture the scene. Then he took a step back and faced the old man across the room.

They squatted across from each other and put the agitated roosters on the floor, unlacing their hoods and repeatedly thrusting them forward, pulling them back. The crowd screamed louder. I could see the blades they'd tied on to the spurs of the poor roosters. Only one of them would survive the fight. Someone blew a whistle, and the crowd quieted down, but only just. One of the bouncers dramatically called out a countdown in Spanish. When he reached the number one, the crowd drew a collective breath. Then the whistle screamed, and the old man and the boy released their cocks, shoving them across the floor at each other. The crowd erupted into a mass of flailing arms and screams.

I looked away from the fight and sketched the crowd. It was them I was interested in, not the pitiful creatures pecking and slicing away at each other. I sketched wide eyes, open mouths, red faces, heads thrown back, hands clutching wads of cash. I sketched the fat slob at the table in the back who collected the bets; I sketched a pair of black clad bouncers standing guard at the door; and, looking across the floor above the fighting animals, I sketched the young man, strong brow, wide brown eyes, perfectly arched eyebrows, a light brown oval birthmark on his left cheek, the shimmer of perspiration on his upper lip, his strong teeth, his prominent Adam's apple as it rose and fell in his throat with each scream, the veins standing out on his neck, his broad shoulder, his pectorals, his biceps. He looked across the floor and locked eyes with me just as the fight was at its most intense — screaming at his rooster; holding my gaze, his eye gleaming. The connection was made. I put away my sketchpad and nodded at him before exiting the chamber.

An hour later I was above ground sharing a joint with the young man, whose name turned out to be Carino, in the tiny Paradiso Bar in a side alley off Alameda Street. It was well past closing time, but I was friends with the owner, a Korean American guy, who had given me a copy of the key to the place. He let me use it for whatever purpose I saw fit, as long as I cleaned up afterward.

Carino and I sat next to each other on the wooden floor, our backs against the wall, huddled over my sketchbook.

'Do I really look like that?' he asked me in Spanish, touching the tip of his index finger to one of the sketches, a close up of his face contorted into a mad scream, his mouth gaping, sharp canines flashing in the firelight, his eyes wide and bulging. I noticed his fingernail was long and shiny as if it had been manicured. Without waiting for an answer, he passed the joint to me and flipped the page.

'Frightening, isn't it?' I said. 'Not to recognize yourself.'

I took a hit on the joint and snuffed it out in the ashtray. I'd had enough. A look of disappointment flashed across his face as I dropped the roach into a baggie and pocketed it. I leaned forward and blew the smoke directly into his mouth, lips touching lips, looking into his deep brown eyes. He leaned back and closed his eyes, holding in the smoke, a crooked smile breaking out on his face as the last of his tension evaporated into the high.

'Why do you do it?' I asked once he'd released the smoke.

He lifted his head in a gesture indicating he hadn't understood my question.

'The cockfight.'

He shrugged. 'He makes us.'

'Who does?'

Carino shook his head.

'Who makes you? The old man?'

He arched an eyebrow and nodded slowly. 'My grandfather. He used to do it in Cuba. Wants me to carry on the family tradition, I guess.'

'What do your parents think?' I asked.

He looked down at the floor for a second and back up at me. 'I don't have parents. They drowned. My little sister too. When we were crossing over. Only my grandfather and I are left.'

'I'm sorry.' I reached out and touched his shoulder. 'When was this?'

'A couple of years ago.' He glanced at my hand, then closed his eyes and slowly shook his head. 'Never mind.'

'It's fine. I'm all ears.'

Carino opened his eyes and stared at me for a few seconds. Then one side of his mouth drew back into a half smile that sent a chill up the length of my spine.

'We could see Key West in the distance,' he said, speaking in an odd monotone. 'The crowds on the pier waiting for the sunset... Everyone on our boat was so excited. A new life. God bless America. Fucking freedom. Then came this big swell from out of nowhere. It capsized us. The next thing I knew, sailors were hauling me onto a Coast Guard ship. My grandfather too. But the rest of them were gone.'

'I'm sorry.'

'You already said that.' He pointed at my pocket. 'Can I have some more? It makes it easier to talk about this stuff.'

'We don't need to talk about it if you don't want. It's getting late anyway.'

'But I want to talk about it.'

He pitched forward and slid the baggy out of my pocket. I grasped his wrist and shook my head. He shrugged and let go of the baggie, letting it drop to the floor, then pressed back against the wall and rubbed his face with his hands.

'How did you end up in LA?' I asked.

'We came to live with my grandfather's brother. Why?'

'Just curious, that's all.'

'How old are you?' he asked after a moment.

'Twenty. Why?'

'Just curious... I'm seventeen.'

I got up from the floor and brought a couple of bottles of Perrier from behind the bar. We sat there sipping water in silence for a while. There was a hollow, haunted look in his eyes that touched me deeply. I picked up my sketchpad and pulled a pencil out of my pocket and spent the next few minutes sketching his eyes, his forehead, the bridge of his nose. Carino sat quietly, his breathing slow and steady. Every so often he glanced at me from under his long lashes. When I finished, I handed him the sketchpad, and he stared at it. He handed it back to me and nodded.

'You should give it up,' I said as I put away my sketchbook. 'The cockfighting. You're too young to be down there. You should be going to school or working a normal job.'

'Normal jobs are for people with normal lives. I don't have a normal life.'

We walked north along Alameda taking in the fresh, early morning air. The construction workers were done for the night and had switched off their lights. The streets were quiet, illuminated only by the street lamps, which shone through a thin fog. Our footsteps echoed off the hard surfaces of the warehouses and concrete sidewalks. When we reached the corner of Alameda and 6th, I pointed at my apartment building.

'I live there,' I said. 'Apartment 3, like the Trinity. That's my bedroom window on the third floor right off the fire escape. If you ever feel like hanging out again, or if you just want to talk, you can find me there, okay?'

Carino nodded.

'Seriously,' I said. 'Come see me, anytime.'

'I have a girlfriend.'

'What about it?'

'I'm not that way.'

'I didn't say you were.'

'Just making sure.'

I held out my hand at Carino. He looked at it for a moment, then he shook it with a firm and steady grip before sprinting back toward the tunnel entrance. I gazed bleary-eyed at his retreating image, feeling suddenly zombified by exhaustion.

A draft of warm air blowing down Alameda startled me out of my daze, and I rubbed the circulation back into my face before jogging over to 6th and clambering up the tree in front of our apartment building. Swinging onto our fire escape, I hiked up the iron stairs to my bedroom window and crawled inside. Five minutes later I was under my covers with a pillow pulled over my head, passing into the dimension of visions.

5

Pater Noster

Fields of landfill spread out at my feet, miles and miles and *miles* of rotting garbage extending to the horizon, and a massive sun was baking it all into a putrid, stinking stew. Out of the field, random bits of garbage came alive, poking up here, skittering out there: iron rods, pieces of ceramic, license plates, exploded tires, they rose up like the dry bones in the prophet Ezekiel's dream and drifted toward each other. From the left of my line of sight, a middle-aged man in fresh-pressed blue coveralls and black boots whom I recognized as my long-estranged father walked onto the scene, a conductor's baton in his hand. He strode to the center of the field, tapped the baton against a podium that materialized before him, and waved his arms. Ever so gently, Strauss' Blue Danube Waltz came up over the scene performed by an unseen orchestra.

Da da de taTA (taTA - taTA); Da da de taTA (taTA - taTA), and so on.

The animated garbage swirled into several twisters in three-quarter time to the waltz, coaxed upward by the conductor higher, higher, reaching upward into the heavens, but ever rooted to the ground from which they sprang. Then the conductor brought his baton down hard against the podium with a loud crack that echoed over the scene. The music stopped, the podium vanished, the field disappeared. All that remained were seventeen interconnected spires of garbage towering over a dilapidated neighborhood that I knew to be in South Central Los Angeles.

The conductor stuffed the baton into his back pocket, walked past me, and crossed the street. He jerked opened the gate in front of one of the houses across from the towers, a low-slung one-story affair in desperate need of paint, with a rock covered roof, and stucco walls with the chicken wire underneath showing through in patches. I followed him as he walked down the driveway that ran alongside the house and crossed a large garden of weeds to a bungalow — more a garden shed than a proper house — butting up against a wall of concrete blocks that defined the limits of the property.

I poked my head into the bungalow and saw a tiny living room that reminded me of a monastic cell. The aroma of brewing coffee filled the room. The clatter of utensils issued from a doorway leading to a room in the back I assumed to be the kitchen. A moment later the conductor came out carrying a tray with a pot of coffee, two cups, a creamer, a sugar bowl, and two tiny spoons. He set it all on a side table and poured coffee into both cups, then took a sip, closing his eyes and smiling, looking like someone on the verge of nirvana. I sat across from him and waited for him to open his eyes.

'Stop that!' my mother's voice echoed in my head.

The dream dissipated and I sat up and found myself facing her ghostly image standing at the foot of my bed, dressed in white and wearing a tiara of blood-red roses. In her right hand she held a long cigar, its burning end glowing angrily in the semi-darkness of my bedroom. She extended it toward me. A trail of smoke from its tip swirled heavenward.

'Let go of him,' she said.

'It was just a dream, Mamá.'

'Dreams kill, mijo. Take back control.'

She took a deep drag on the cigar and exhaled the protective smoke in my direction as her image faded, and I was left staring at the life-size print of the crucified Christ nailed onto the wall opposite my bed.

'Yes, Mamá ...'

I spoke the words into the darkness of the empty room and breathed in the remnants of the aromatic smoke. Then I hauled myself out of bed and stepped onto the fire escape in my underwear to watch the sky lighten with the advancing dawn. Two blocks east of our tenement, the top span of the 6th Street Bridge, deserted at this time of the morning, glowed warmly in the reflected light. In about an hour, the first trickle of cars entering the city would roll across it, eventually turning into a surging river of rumbling traffic that would last over twelve hours. But at that time of the morning, it was just me and the bridge.

'Come, my son,' it said, its voice softer than a whisper. A sudden puff of cool air kicked up and caressed my body, prickling my skin.

Climbing back into my room, I tugged on a pair of white linen trousers and a black tank top, scrambled down the fire escape, and jogged up the road to the bridge. Then I dropped onto the service ledge that skirted its lower half, right below the road, and curled up against one of the iron support grids to smoke a hand-rolled cigarette. The cool concrete of the ledge throbbed gently, and I closed my eyes and absorbed the vibrations, allowing myself to think again about my father, for just a passing moment, before taking control and forcing him out of my mind. I opened moist eyes and stared out over the dry river channel.

'Don't fret, my son,' the bridge whispered. 'I'm all the family you need.'

'I need Celia, too.' I took another drag on my cigarette. 'And she needs me.'

'Celia needs no one. And once your training is complete, she will release you.'

I flicked the cigarette over the ledge and watched it float down to the bank of the river channel.

'She's my mother, for God's sake. She'd never abandon me. Not like him.'

'No, but she *will* release you, as all parents should their children. And when she does, I'll still be here for you. Just as I was when he left all those years ago. Until they tear me down.'

A chill ran through me, and I slowly rose to my feet, reaching out a hand to steady myself against one of the support beams. 'What do you mean?'

My question was met by silence.

'What do you mean until they tear you down?' I repeated.

'Todo esto se acaba.'

'No,' I said. 'I won't let that happen.'

'We'll talk more later, my son. The day has started. Go forth. Everything begins now.'

6

Temptation

Later that afternoon, I was sitting on the landing outside my bedroom window working up some of my sketches, the bridge's last words still echoing in my mind. The rush hour had started, and 6th Street was now a one-way river of cars grinding past our building, headed over the viaduct away from the city. I needed the energy of that traffic to prime my brain. It was just the right density and moved at the ideal pace. The rumble of engines, the smell of exhaust, the occasional blast of a car horn borne of frustration, these were the things that stoked the flames of my imagination. And out of those flames flickered images of my nightly wanderings and the dreams they inspired.

I called up the memory of Concha chatting up the middle-aged man in the bar, my pencil poised over my sketchpad, ready to apply the first stroke, when I noticed a young woman dodging traffic from across the street, her hand held up as if she had the power to stop the forward movement of the cars. I immediately recognized Beatrice Schein. Sunglasses, white blouse, blue-and-green checkered skirt, her auburn hair tied back with a sapphire scarf. She mounted the sidewalk and glanced at a slip of paper in her hand, then she scanned the buildings and moved toward ours. She hadn't noticed me on the fire escape. When she reached the doorway, she lifted her sunglasses and peered at the buzzer panel, from which the names had long peeled away. Then she stepped back and looked side to side, puzzling out what to do next.

'Are you looking for me?' I called down from the fire escape.

Beatrice looked up, squinting one eye against the afternoon sun. Her face looked radiant as it reflected the warm light.

'Virgilio?'

I set aside my sketchpad and slid down the fire escape, dropping onto the sidewalk beside her.

'What are you doing here?' I flashed a smile to soften the tone of my question.

She held out the slip of paper with my address carefully printed on it. I recognized Lucinda's handwriting.

'I don't know if you heard. But I bought all the paintings you were exhibiting.'

I took the paper out of her hands, stared at it for a moment, and turned it over. 'Yes, I heard. Thank you.'

'I wanted to talk to you last night. But you ran out so quickly. I asked the director of the center for your home address. I hope you don't mind.'

I shrugged and handed back the piece of paper.

Beatrice smiled tightly and looked around at the deserted, weedy sidewalk in contrast to the mass of humanity rumbling past us in exhaust-spewing cars. An RTD bus driver laid on his horn as a late-model Ford Pinto edged in front him, the standoff halting the lane closest to where we were standing. She looked back at me.

'Is there someplace we could go for a coffee?'

'There's no place around here, sorry.' I glanced at my wristwatch. 'Besides, I've got gymnastics at 5:30.'

She nodded and pulled a folded newspaper out of her purse. 'I don't know if you've seen this, but there's a nice write-up about the show in this afternoon's *Herald Examiner*. Anne's going to do a story in *Los Angeles Magazine*, and she wants to feature a couple of artists in it, including you.'

I don't know why exactly, but I started to feel sorry for the woman, standing there in her expensive clothes, designer handbag, and perfect hair. Clearly, she was wealthy and self-assured, but at the same time, she seemed needy.

'You don't look impressed,' she said, slipping the newspaper back into her purse.

'Where are you parked?' I asked.

She raised her eyes at me.

'I know a place on the other side of the bridge where we can talk. They have decent coffee and good Mexican food. The chef has a Cordon Bleu certificate. We'd have to drive there.'

A few minutes later we were rumbling down the side streets in her black Porsche Carrera. It smelled brand new and still had the temporary license plates. I pointed the way to try to avoid traffic as best as possible. We wound past abandoned warehouses, boarded up buildings, piles of rotting garbage, up and around the 4th Street overpass until we finally rejoined traffic on 1st Street. I pointed at the arts center as we drove past it.

'My second home.'

Beatrice glanced at the building and smiled.

* * *

We sat across from each other at a table in the back of the restaurant where it was quiet. The server brought us coffees. Beatrice picked up her cup, took in the aroma and tried a sip. She gave a quick nod of approval and placed the cup back on the saucer.

'I'm used to stronger stuff than what they serve in most restaurants,'

I said, taking a sip. 'But this place isn't bad.'

'Why is that?'

'They make it with proper espresso here. The chef studied in Paris, so he tries to Frenchify everything, the coffee included.'

'I meant, why are you used to stronger coffee?'

'Oh, sorry. I'm used to my mother's coffee. She's from Cuba.'

Beatrice's eyes went wide. 'Is she really? I thought you were Mexican.'

'Half Mexican,' I said. 'My mom's from Cuba; my dad was from Mexico.'

'Was?'

'Yeah, he abandoned us when I was a kid. Long story.'

'Oh, I'm sorry. That must have been very hard, I imagine. Are you still in contact?'

'Next question.'

The server brought a basket of warm, handmade flour tortillas cut into quarters and a couple of small bowls of green and red salsa. She took our orders and withdrew into the kitchen.

'I'm sorry. I didn't mean to pry,' Beatrice said after a moment of silence.

'No worries. I just don't like to talk about personal stuff like that with strangers.'

'No, of course not.'

I pushed aside the coffee and waved down the waiter.

'I suddenly feel like having a beer. How about you?'

'I'm driving.'

I laughed. 'Live a little. You can sit out the rush hour. Besides, one beer won't put you over the limit.' I ordered two Coronas from the waiter and grinned at Beatrice.

'I thought you had to go to the gym.'

'I'm going to make an exception today. I don't normally do that. But you drove out all the way from — where exactly?'

'I live in the Westside.'

'Beverly Hills, Bel Air, Brentwood?'

The server returned with two open bottles of beer and poured them into our glasses.

'Holmby Hills. You know the Westside?'

'Don't act so surprised. I didn't just crawl out from under a rock.'

'No, of course not. I didn't mean to suggest that.' She cleared her throat and raised her glass. 'In any case, Virgilio, a toast.'

'What are we toasting?'

'The future, I hope.'

I put down my glass and cocked my head.

'I'll be honest, Virgilio. I've been on the lookout for quite some time for an artist like yourself. Someone whose career I can help mold. Someone I can bring to the attention of the art world. I think you're the perfect candidate. You've got the talent; you're eloquent, you're nice-looking. All the elements are there for a fantastic rags-to-riches story. I can make that all happen.'

Her face lit up as she spoke with increasing intensity. She leaned across the table, holding my gaze with her beautiful violet eyes. She was interrupted mid-sentence by the server who brought our dishes, veggie gorditas for me, sea bass in cilantro sauce for Beatrice, and a couple of steaming sharing bowls of yellow rice, mashed pinto beans, and a basket of corn tortillas. I raised my glass.

'Here's to an excellent meal,' I said.

Beatrice tapped her glass against mine.

'And to the future?'

'We'll see,' I answered. 'First, tell me something about yourself.'

Beatrice spent the rest of the meal telling me about her family and herself. How she was born in Geneva to a Swiss Italian father and an American mother who had met each other in university. How her father was from an old private banking family with several sons and was now in charge of the North American branch. How she, Beatrice, was educated in American schools in Switzerland before they'd come to Los Angeles in 1971 when she was ten years old and later studied museology at Wellesley.

It went on and on, over one beer, and another, through the starter, main course, a plate of flan, and another coffee. It was as if I'd turned on a spigot I couldn't shut off — no matter how many times I politely interjected a comment, looked to the side, glanced at my watch, went to the restroom. I can't say I paid attention to every detail, there were so many, but it was clear to me Beatrice Schein felt very privileged indeed; better, in fact, than the rest of us mere mortals down here below.

Then she turned to her plans for me. How it was a pity my talent should go forever unnoticed here in the barrio (her words), and how she could help bring me to the attention of the great and powerful of the art world. She invoked the names of Salvador Dali and Vincent Van Gogh, neither of whom we would have heard of had it not been for Gala in the case of Dali; Theo in the case of Van Gogh. It was clear: she had spotted me from the corner of heaven she inhabited and had descended to rescue me from the hell she imagined I was living. Then came the rub.

'Of course, I'd have to know quite a lot more about you.' She smiled at me over the last bite of flan, her fork hovering in the air. 'There's no question about your talent. But I'll have to know whether you're personally suited before I invest in you.'

I smiled back at her. 'What do you mean?' I made sure there was the right amount of ice in my smile.

'You're an unknown. We need to know more about you, your personal story, where you came from, how you spend your days. That would be for the PR side of things.'

She put the piece of flan in her mouth and slid the fork onto the empty dessert plate. I noticed it didn't make a sound as the metal made contact with the ceramic.

'Who's we?'

'My friend Anne Levine, the art critic for the *Herald*. She'd be part of the project as well. We'd also need to know something about your habits, the people you associate with. We can't afford any surprises, if you know what I mean. I'm talking about skeletons in closets.'

She lifted a finger at the server who was speeding past our table on her way to greet a couple entering the restaurant and pointed at her empty coffee cup.

'I'm an artist. We have skeletons. And they're not all in closets. You did mention Van Gogh a half hour ago, didn't you?'

Beatrice waved her hand dismissively. 'For instance, I understand from the director of the center that the woman you were with at the opening, the African-American one in the charming Japanese outfit, how do I put this, that she's not actually a woman. That she performs in some shady downtown cabaret.'

I set down my coffee cup with a loud clatter.

'She's a woman. And why were you asking about her? I thought it was me you're interested in.'

'I was simply curious to know if you and she were a couple. The director volunteered the rest. It's of no concern to me, of course. I don't know why I even mentioned it.'

'With respect, Miss, it's hands off my friends and family, if you don't mind. Anything you need to know, I'll tell you. Otherwise, it's no deal.'

Beatrice arched an eyebrow at me. She lifted her empty cup to receive the coffee the server poured, then took a sip and nodded.

'I'm single, by the way, if that's what you wanted to know.' I glanced at my watch. 'I'm going to have to get going.' I reached into my pocket and pulled out my wallet. Beatrice held up her hand.

'This is on me, please. I'll give you a ride back. And I'm sorry if I offended you.'

'No worries. Thanks for dinner. I'll find my way back.'

'When can we meet again? May I have your telephone number? Also, Anne wants to set up a time for an interview.'

'I don't have a phone, sorry. I'm at the center every evening from 6:30 till around 9:00, except for Sundays. So if you or Anne want to drop by, just call ahead a couple of days and leave a message for me.'

She rose and kissed me on both cheeks, Euro style. Then she smiled and gave my hand a little squeeze.

'I do hope this is the start of something,' she said. 'And, it's Beatrice, not Miss.'

'Thanks again for dinner. Next time it's on me.'

I exited the restaurant through a door in the back that opened onto a small parking lot and connecting alley. It was already seven o'clock, and I was feeling tipsy after the three or four beers I'd had over dinner. So I decided, for the first time in I don't know how long, to skip the center that night. I'd been working hard on the exhibition and felt I'd earned a break. So I changed course and headed in the direction of the tenement on Los Angeles Street where Concha lived.

I kept thinking about Beatrice and her offer. Anyone I knew would have jumped at the mere suggestion of a wealthy patron proposing to turn them into a darling of the art world. But I didn't like the fact Beatrice Schein seemed more interested in me than in my art. And though she hadn't actively flirted with me yet, her offer might have sexual strings attached, which I wouldn't be able to tolerate. In any case, the picture that kept coming to mind was of Satan's temptation of Christ as they viewed Jerusalem from the pinnacle of the Temple. I stepped off the main road into a side street, pulled a pad out of my backpack, and quickly sketched that image.

When I arrived at Concha's place, she was about to jump into the shower. She pointed at a bag of tortilla chips and a jar of nacho cheese dip sitting atop a white lacquer desk surrounded by a mountain of sample lipsticks and makeup kits. I'd once seen a photograph from World War II of a Berlin cosmetics shop that had been hit by a bomb dropped from an Allied aircraft, its shattered contents spilled onto the sidewalk. That was Concha's make up desk. Above the desk shone an old-school vanity mirror framed by twelve oversize lightbulbs, half of which were burned out. I switched off the mirror lights and sat on Concha's bed while I waited for her to come out of the bathroom. The next thing I knew Concha was standing over me wearing a blue satin bathrobe and slippers and towel-drying her hair. I sat up and patted a spot on the bed. Concha slipped in next to me and lowered her head to my shoulder. We stayed that way for a few minutes, neither of us saying anything, then she looked at me.

'What's happened, mijo?'

I kissed her on the cheek, then sat up and rested my back against the wall. 'Nothing.'

She shook her head, grabbed a newspaper from her nightstand and dropped it into my lap.

'Congratulations, *mentiroso*.'

I picked up the paper and scanned Anne Levine's story about the exhibition. Concha had circled the part that mentioned the acquisition of my paintings with an eyebrow pencil. I handed the paper back to her.

'Lucky me,' I said.

'It's not luck, *cabron*. You're a great artist. I can't believe you didn't tell me about this.'

'You were there, remember?'

She shook the newspaper at me. 'I'm talking about this, *cabrito*. Your name in the papers.'

I took it out of her hands, folded it neatly, and put it on the nightstand on the other side of the bed, out of her reach.

'I only found out about it myself this afternoon. I'm still processing it. Sorry.'

'And what are you doing here at this time anyway? You're supposed to be at the center, aren't you?'

She got up from the bed and shook out her hair, then grabbed a brush and passed it through her hair, staring at me at the same time.

'I needed a break. What do you say we go to the beach?'

'The beach? At this time?'

'Yeah, we could grab the all-nighter to Santa Monica and sit on the sand like in the old days. I love the beach at night.'

Concha dropped the brush on the nightstand and put her hand on my forehead. I backed away.

'What are you doing?'

'Just checking if you're running a *fiebre*, mijo. You're talking crazy.'

I stood and wrapped my arms around Concha's waist. 'It's not crazy. I just need a little getaway. A change of scenery.' I kissed her forehead. 'Come on, preciosa. Do this for me.'

Concha kissed me lightly on the lips, then backed away and moved to her makeup desk.

'I can't, mijo. I'm sorry. I'm working tonight. Maybe on Thursday if nothing else comes up.'

I watched Concha pucker up at the mirror to apply a top-coat of lipstick as she readied herself for another midnight prowl; I realized then how much I feared for her. I'd saved her once before when we were in high school when she was still known as Jesús. She'd been on the brink of committing suicide when I found her one afternoon whimpering behind the library with a bruised eye, the victim of a band of bullies. She was two years older than me. I was a freshman; she was a junior. In those days, she looked like a boy and dressed like a boy. But everything about her screamed otherwise. And this enraged the bullies who tormented her to no end. The afternoon I found her, I took her to the infirmary, and we visited the principal's office where I helped her lodge a complaint. She feared a reprisal, and I swore to her I'd be there to protect her. I did better than that.

One afternoon, I followed the main bully home, a Chicano kid from over the bridge, and waited across the street until he came out in the evening. I followed him for a couple of blocks, a baseball bat in my hand. As he rounded the corner onto a quiet street, I pushed him into an alley and beat the shit out of him. When I finished, I peered into his bloody face and swore I'd kill him if he or any of his friends ever so much as breathed on Jesús again. I punctuated my threat by stomping on his balls before stealing out of the alley. And that was the end of the harassment. Still, I never forgot to watch my back.

From that day until the day she dropped out of school in the middle of her senior year, Jesús and I were inseparable. I would meet her at her house in the mornings, accompany her to classes when I could, and escort her home in the afternoons. Everyone was convinced we were a thing. But it was never like that with us.

As if hearing my thoughts, Concha pivoted around and looked at me, a questioning look in her eye. I gave a little shrug and shook my head. I'd saved her once before, from the bullies that tormented her. That was easy. I wasn't so sure I'd be able to save her from herself.

7

Last Supper

'*Oye*, Santos, you just missed a call from your groupie,' one of the muralists called out as I stepped into the art center the next afternoon.

'My groupie?'

She pointed a paintbrush in the direction of the exhibition space. 'Yes, papi, your groupie. Lucinda took a message.'

Sexto intercepted me as I sped across the floor to Lucinda's office. 'Hey, vato, you're still coming over tonight, right?'

'Of course. I wouldn't miss it.'

'I've been shucking corn for two days. So you'd better *not* miss it. Plus, my abuelita's dying to meet you.' He held out a slip of paper. 'Here's where I live.'

I pocketed his address and gave him a quick hug, then excused myself and headed to Lucinda's office. I found her at her desk hunched over a typewriter. Her dyed red hair was pulled into a short ponytail, and she was wearing her trademark dark blue coveralls and black pumps. I knocked on the doorpost, and she swiveled around and took off her black horn-rimmed glasses.

'I heard you have a message for me,' I said.

She ripped a page out of her message pad and, smiling broadly, held it out to me. 'Beatrice Schein called. She's arranged a lunch meeting on Monday between you and Anne Levine, her contact at the *Herald Examiner*, for a possible feature story. Congratulations, mijo.'

I took the message slip out of her hand and examined it, feeling my heart speeding up as I processed the additional information — a meeting with Anne Levine in the Polo Lounge at the Beverly Hills Hotel.

'She said to make sure you wear a blazer and a tie, and no sneakers.'

I looked up at Lucinda, who was now standing.

'They have a strict dress code,' she said.

'I know. I've been there before.'

'You seem preoccupied, mijo. Is something wrong?'

The corners of Lucinda's mouth were turning down. So I forced a smile.

'No, not at all. It's just taking some time for it all to sink in. I'm not used to so many positive things happening to me all at once.' I drew a deep breath and was relieved to see Lucinda's face light up again.

'You deserve every bit of it, mijo,' she said. 'Never doubt that.'

* * *

As I approached our tenement, I was surprised to see the figure of a young man huddled on the front steps of our building. It was already dark, and the stoop where he was sitting was just outside a circle of light cast by the street lamp. Given the increasing number of assaults on residents in our neighborhood, I slowed my pace and cleared my throat to announce my presence from a safe enough distance in case I had to beat a quick retreat. In response, he jumped to his feet into the lamplight. I immediately recognized Carino. He had pulled back his long hair into a neat ponytail and was wearing a freshly ironed, dark blue button shirt, a new pair of 501s, and spotless white tennis shoes. I could smell the scent of Fahrenheit on his neck as he pulled me into a tight hug and then released me, staring into my eyes with an earnestness that took me aback.

'I've been waiting for you for all afternoon,' he said.

'Sorry about that.' I averted my eyes from his intense gaze and moved toward our building. 'I wasn't expecting you.'

'You said I could come see you any time,' he said.

'Of course.' I flashed my teeth as he pulled alongside me. 'You're always welcome. It's just that I've got a thing to go to tonight.'

A cloud of disappointment drifted across his face. 'What kind of a thing?' The light of the streetlamp reflected in the shine of tears pooling in his eyes.

'It's a family thing.'

'Oh.' An awkward silence hung in the air, broken only by the occasional rumble of cars heading down Alameda in the direction of South Central. After a moment, he spoke again: 'But I wanted to hang out with you and talk some more — like you said I could.'

I regarded him out of the corner of my eye as I slid out the keys to our building from the pocket of my jeans. His body was unnaturally rigid, every muscle in his body spring-loaded, the muscles of his jaw pulsating.

'I still have some time before I have to take off,' I said, hoping to defuse the tension. 'We can hang out until then. Then we'll figure out another time when we can spend the whole evening together.' I squeezed his arm and felt him relax into the gesture. 'Does that work?'

Carino nodded and flashed a half smile.

'Great; come on up.' I pushed open the door to our building and ushered him inside.

Carino's eyes went wide as he crossed the threshold into my apartment.

'This is where the magic happens,' I said, dropping my backpack onto the sofa and pulling out a chair for him at the kitchen table.

Carino wandered around the living room gawking at the statues and paintings of the various saints. He stopped in front of the fruit-laden altar pushed up against the wall separating my bedroom from my mother's, on which burned several freshly lit votive candles.

He spun around and stared at me. 'You're a Santero?'

I patted the back of his chair. 'Over here.'

He crossed the room to the table and sat side-saddle in the chair, still staring at me, waiting for a response.

'Not me,' I answered. 'It's my mother.'

'She lives here?'

I nodded. 'We live together.'

Carino looked around the apartment, an absent look in his eye. Then he turned back to me and said in a low voice, 'My mother believed in it too.' He extended his hand in the direction of the altar. 'This stuff reminds me of home...back in Cuba.' Tears filled his eyes again. He swiped at them with the back of his hand and drew a deep breath.

I grabbed a Coke out of the refrigerator, served it to him in a glass over some ice, and sat next to him.

'Where is she?' he asked, staring at the glass.

'Who?'

'Your mother.' He cocked his head at me. 'You said you live together. Where is she?'

'She's at work. Why?'

'Can I meet her?'

'Why do you want to meet her?'

Carino shrugged and sipped his Coke. 'I just do.' He drained the glass and set it down on the table with a loud thud. 'Can I?'

We stared at each other without speaking for a few seconds. It reminded me of the staring contests my friends and I used to have in grade school; the last one to blink won the game. The longer it went on, the wider Carino's eyes grew. After a couple of minutes, I thought the better of it and gave in, if only to wrest control of what was becoming an absurd impasse. 'Of course, you can meet her,' I said, forcing a smile. 'I'll invite you back over when she has a day off.' I refilled his glass and grabbed my book bag. 'I'll be right back.'

I left him at the kitchen table and went to my bedroom to change out of my street clothes into something nicer for dinner. As I was rummaging around in my closet for a pair of linen trousers, I heard the creak of my door and turned to find Carino standing in the doorway, staring at me in just my underwear, an empty glass in his hand.

'What are you doing?' he asked.

'I'm changing clothes.' I straightened up and stared back at him.

Carino gazed at the sacred heart tattoo inked on my chest, his mouth hanging slightly open. He lifted his glass at me. 'That's beautiful.'

'Thanks.' I gestured with my head toward my bed. 'You can wait there if you want.'

Carino sat on the edge of the bed and continued staring at me. Turning away, I stepped into a pair of black linen trousers and pulled on a white button shirt, buttoning it up to the top. Then I sat next to him on the bed as I slipped into a pair of penny loafers. Carino scooted back on the bed and reclined against my pillows.

'Come on,' I said, hopping up and moving to the door. Carino narrowed his eyes at me and stood, and I snatched the empty glass out of his hand. 'It's your lucky night! I'm going to take you to my favorite place in all the world.'

Ten minutes later we were sitting on the ledge under the 6th Street Bridge, our legs dangling over the precipice, a few hundred feet above the dry viaduct. The concrete of the bridge was still warm from the day, and it vibrated with the last of the outbound traffic flowing over it. I offered Carino a cigarette, but he shook his head.

'I wouldn't mind a joint,' he said.

'No joint tonight,' I said. 'Next time.'

Carino shrugged and leaned back against one of the metal spans.

'So, what did you want to talk about?' I asked.

He pivoted his head toward me, a deadpan expression on his face, then closed his eyes and shook his head. 'Never mind.'

'Does it have anything to do with what we were talking about the other night?'

'Maybe.'

'About quitting the cockfight?'

Carino lurched forward, which made my heart jump, and my hand shot out at his chest to keep him from falling over the edge. He grasped my wrist and held it tight.

'What the fuck was that?' My body was shaking from the fright he gave me.

'I can't quit the cockfight. It would kill my grandfather.'

'Okay, okay, just...' I gently pressed him back against the span. 'Rest there. It's a long way down.'

'I could really use a joint, man.'

'I don't have any on me, sorry.'

Carino rubbed his face with his hands and pushed back against the span. 'Never mind. Anyway, if I tell you something, do you promise not to tell anyone?'

'Your secrets are safe with me, I promise.'

'I need advice, and you're, like, the big brother I never had. And this is really personal. So I need to know I can trust you.'

'You can.'

'Swear to me.'

'Yes, I swear. I won't tell anyone.'

He nodded, glanced around, then dipped his head toward me and spoke in a low voice. 'I used to have a girlfriend, back in Cuba...'

'Okay.'

'We broke up before I left.'

'It's sort of difficult to be in a relationship when you never see the other person. So it's understandable.'

'But I haven't had another girlfriend since then. And that was over two years ago.'

'And that worries you?'

Carino nodded.

'You obviously still miss her. Plus, you've been busy, I guess. What with the following your grandfather all around and the cockfighting. And you're still grieving about your family. You just need to give it some time. Let things happen naturally.'

'I don't think it's just that.' He rocked onto his knees and leaned in toward me, and I thought it best to fight the instinct to move away. 'Remember when I told you the other night that I'm not that way?' he asked.

'Yeah, I remember.'

'Well, I think I actually *might* be that way.'

I took a drag on my cigarette and exhaled the smoke out of the side of my mouth. 'Why are you telling me this, Carino?'

Carino rested his hand on my knee, and I looked down at it.

'What's wrong?' he said.

'A lot.' I scooted away from him. 'First, you're seventeen, and I'm twenty. Second, *I'm* not that way. And even if I was, I'm not available.'

Carino pulled back his hand and his eyes became hard. 'But I thought...'

'Look, I'm happy to be your friend and to hang out with you from time to time, and to give you big-brother advice whenever you need it. But that's it.' I stood up. 'If you're okay with that, then we can keep seeing each other.'

I checked my watch and saw that I had just enough time to get to Sexto's on time if I walked quickly. I grabbed Carino by the wrist and pulled him onto his feet. 'I've got to run now, if that's okay.'

He looked out over the riverbed for a moment, then looked back at me. 'Yeah, sure thing, bro.'

He followed me up to the street, then we parted ways without another word, Carino walking with his head down in the direction of the tunnels, and me speeding across the bridge to East Los Angeles toward Sexto's.

8

Judas

The Santa Ana winds had kicked up fiercely by the time I arrived at Sexto's ramshackle craftsman-style house, with its massive wrap-around porch and large flakes of dark blue paint peeling off rotting wood, a bottle of Rioja in one hand and bouquet of pink dahlias for Sexto's grandmother in the other. Although he'd invited me many times to what he lovingly referred to as his Chicano castle, this was the first time I'd ever actually visited him, and, for some reason, it broke my heart to see the state of it.

Just as I raised my hand to knock on the front door, it swung open and a smiling Sexto popped out and enveloped me in a sweet-smelling bear hug, unbelievably lifting me off the ground despite the fact I outweighed him by a good thirty pounds. He pulled me into the house, which I was surprised to see was the total opposite of what I'd seen outside, freshly painted walls the color of a yellow gourd, complemented by a polished hardwood floor and matching cherrywood crossbeams on its high ceilings. The walls were decorated with folkloric hangings and crafts typical of the Yucatan Peninsula, which was where Sexto's family was from originally, and the comfortable-looking hand-wrought wooden furniture was understated and covered in multicolored, woven blankets.

The warm smell of tamales, freshly made tortillas, and *mole*-stewed meat wafting from the kitchen filled the room.

'Dude, I can't believe you're finally here.' Sexto stepped back and grinned his gap-toothed smile at me, looking weirdly preppie in a pair of black jeans and a red Polo shirt. 'Come meet my abuelita. She's been so excited all afternoon.'

He took me by the arm and led me across the front room into the large kitchen, where his grandmother was sitting at the kitchen table, staring absently into a random corner of the room. She looked to be in her eighties, dressed in a paisley housedress and slippers, Her grey hair was pinned up, and she looked thin and frail. The skin that overlay her prominent cheekbones was thin and wrinkled as crepe paper.

'Abuelita, this is my friend Virgilio, from the art center, the one I told you about.' Sexto kissed his grandmother on the cheek and gently lifted her head by the chin, pivoting her head in my direction. As soon as her eyes met mine, she straightened up and smiled and extended her hand toward me.

'It's a pleasure to meet you, Señora. Happy birthday.' I took her thin hand and gave it a little squeeze, then held out the bouquet. 'These are for you.'

She smiled at me and looked at Sexto. 'He's very nice, mijo. Very handsome.'

'He's a great artist, too, Abuelita,' Sexto said, taking the flowers and the wine and placing them on the kitchen counter. 'Some rich lady bought a bunch of his paintings at the exhibition, and now she want to do a story about him for a magazine.'

My head snapped up at his mention of the magazine piece, and Sexto responded with a wink. 'Word gets around fast. You'll have to tell us more about it over dinner.In the meantime' — he pulled out a chair for me across from his grandmother — 'sit here and chat with Abuelita while I finish preparing dinner.'

As soon as I sat down, Sexto's grandmother's eyes lit up, and she leaned across the table, placing her thin hands on mine. She proceeded to fill me in on her family history while Sexto fretted in the background over the various pots he was juggling as he finished preparing dinner, adding to the conversation by interjecting a comment or two from time to time. I learned how she and her husband and their young son, Sexto's father, had left Mexico in the 1940s. Soon after their arrival in Los Angeles, her husband had suffered a stroke that left him bedridden for years. Sexto's father set up a body shop in East Los Angeles, which did amazingly well and made it possible for him to buy this house, where he lived with his parents until his father finally passed away.

'My poor son,' she said, her eyes filling with tears. 'He put off marrying to take care of his father. He was an angel.'

'Now, now, Abuelita,' Sexto said, as he set the table. 'This is supposed to be a celebration. 'Virgilio doesn't need to hear all that drama.' He dried her cheeks with the back of his hand and kissed her.

'I don't mind,' I said, smiling warmly at his grandmother. 'It's good to reminisce sometimes, right? Birthdays are always good for that.'

Sexto straightened up and discreetly shook his head at me, and I immediately regretted saying anything. His grandmother reached out and took hold of his hand. 'This one's an angel, too,' she said, pulling him close and leaning her head against him. 'Both his parents died in a car accident when he was only thirteen, and he's been taking care of me ever since.'

Sexto's eyes met mine, and he flashed a sad smile. And in that moment, my admiration for that cocky, oversexed teenage art center assistant shot through the roof. After a moment of awkward silence, I raised my wineglass and toasted Sexto's grandmother. Then Sexto put on some traditional *trovas* to lift the mood, and we spent the next couple of hours eating the delicious meal Sexto had prepared, drinking way too much wine, and even managing to do a bit of dancing in the front room — including Sexto's abuelita. By the end of the evening, she was listing to one side on the sofa, a serene smile on her deeply lined face.

'I should get her to bed,' Sexto said, leaning over her and caressing her forehead, a little frown playing on his lips.

I squeezed his arm. 'Do you need help?'

'Nah, I'm all right.' He helped her off the sofa and walked with her to the stairs leading up to the bedrooms. He glanced over his shoulder at me and said, 'I'll be down in a moment. Just kick back and have some more wine.'

Feeling suddenly exhausted, I gathered up my coat and backpack and readied myself to go while I waited for Sexto to come back downstairs. After the festive atmosphere of the party, the house felt strangely quiet, almost too quiet. Checking my watch, I was surprised to see it was almost midnight.

I wondered what was taking Sexto so long, as I was really keen to get going. So I approached the stairwell and strained to hear what was going on upstairs. But all was still as death, which, for some reason, made me a bit anxious.

Stumbling back to the living room, I calmed myself by mentally composing a painting based on the room, which nearly always worked for me. As I cast about the room, seeking a point of focus, a swift movement in the shadows caught my eye, just beyond the front window on the porch. I pulled back the thin curtain and peered outside.

'What are you doing?' I heard at my back.

Turning around, I saw Sexto standing at the foot of the stairs, his head cocked to one side.

'I thought I saw something,' I said.

'You're not going yet, are you?' He pointed at the backpack hanging off my shoulder. 'I didn't get a chance to show you my bungalow.' He jerked his thumb toward the back of the house. 'It's like my own private apartment.'

'I'll come back some other time,' I said, pulling him into a hug. 'I've got that meeting tomorrow with Anne the magazine lady, so I need to get some sleep. But thanks for inviting me over. It was great.'

Sexto smiled broadly and pulled me into another hug and surprised me by planting a big kiss on my cheek. I retreated a bit and stared at him, and Sexto shrugged. 'Blame it on the wine,' he said with a smirk.

As I descended the steps of his porch to the street, someone moved out of the shadow of a large pepper tree on Sexto's front lawn and onto the sidewalk in front of me, blocking my way. It was Carino, who took up a confrontational stance, legs wide apart, his hands shoved deep in his pockets.

'You said you were going to a family thing,' he said in a low voice bordering on a growl.

'What are you doing here?' I said, readying myself for anything.

'You told me you couldn't hang out because you were going to a family thing, so I followed you to see if it was true.'

'You've been here the whole time?'

'That's right, and I saw everything, you liar.' Carino took a step toward me.

'What the hell are you talking about?' I asked.

He raised his arm and pointed a finger at the house. 'You were kissing that guy.'

I spun around and saw Sexto stepping off his porch and coming toward us, a baseball bat hanging loosely from his hand.

'Who is this, Virgilio?' Sexto asked.

'Who the fuck are *you*?' Carino responded, lifting his head at the baseball bat. 'And why were you kissing him?' He pointed at me.

'Just in case you hadn't noticed' — Sexto raised the baseball bat over his head, and my hand shot out to hold him back — 'this is my house.'

'Hang on a second, both of you,' I said, pulling down Sexto's arm.

'First of all, Sexto, this is Carino; he works in the tunnels. I met him the other night.'

'Don't go telling him my business,' Carino shouted.

'I said hang on!' I shouted back. Both Carino and Sexto reacted by falling silent, waiting for me to continue. I indicated Sexto with a nod of my head. 'Sexto's a friend of mine, and he invited me to his grandmother's birthday party, which I'm sure you must have seen if you've been spying on me all night. So it actually *was* a family thing.'

'You mean, he's been here the whole time?' Sexto said, his hand gripping the baseball bat tightly again.

Carino shook his head and glared at me. 'This is your fault, you know. You're the one who told me we could hang out any time.'

'Are you fricking kidding me? When I said any time, I didn't mean it literally.'

'Whatever, man.' Carino turned his back to us and moved down the sidewalk. 'Enjoy your life with your faggot boyfriend,' he shouted over his shoulder.

'What the fuck?' Sexto screamed, and he broke into a chase after Carino, the baseball bat held high over his head.

Seeing Sexto coming after him, Carino sprinted down the road, and I chased after them. Carino ran at full speed down the slope of the empty street with the precision of an Olympic pentathlete, while Sexto struggled to keep up, still wielding the bat over his head and gasping for air between screams.

Just as Carino rounded the bend at 1st Street, I caught up with Sexto and grabbed for his arm. Jerking away, he tossed aside the bat, sending it clattering into the gutter, and launched himself down the north sidewalk in pursuit of Carino, slaloming around randomly placed newspaper vending machines and overflowing garbage cans. Carino countered by dashing across the street to the opposite sidewalk at the 1st Street Bridge, making for the retaining wall, and Sexto tore after him

— straight into the path of a shiny red Buick low-rider that appeared from out of nowhere.

The screech of slammed-on brakes split the night and the air filled with the stink of burning rubber on asphalt as the Buick lurched to a stop inches from Sexto. The driver, a pissed-off looking thirtysomething *cholo* with a tattoo-splashed bald head, white tank and khaki cut-offs, jumped out of his car and pitched a half-full beer bottle at Sexto who had just mounted the sidewalk, hitting him square in the middle of his back and dropping him. Seeing what was unfolding just inches away from him, Carino flashed a smirk and clambered down the side of the bridge to the access ladder leading to the riverbed.

I snatched up the baseball bat and ran across the road, swooping onto the sidewalk just in time to face off with the cholo who was swaggering toward Sexto with murder in his eyes, his fists tightened, the muscles on his bare arms pulsating.

'Get back in your car and drive away,' I said, gripping the baseball bat, with one hand at either end, readying myself to use it if necessary.

The cholo drew up and looked first at me, then at Sexto who was scrambling onto his knees and moaning in pain, then back at me. He sneered and drew a switchblade out of his khakis, flipping it open and holding it out. I shifted the bat and held it at a forty-five-degree angle across my chest.

'Come on, man, take a breath. He's just a kid,' I said. 'Leave him to me.'

The cholo took another look at Sexto, who was now sitting on the sidewalk hugging his knees, blinking away tears, his upper lip trembling. I noted a change in the cholo's breathing and a slight relaxing of the bicep of the arm holding the switchblade. Taking advantage of the momentary lull in tension, I raised my head at his car.

'Put away the weapon, man. Let's call it a night.'

The cholo glanced back at his car, nodded absently, then pushed closed the blade and pocketed the weapon.

I nudged Sexto with my leg. 'Tell him you're sorry.'

Sexto glanced up at me and rolled his eyes.

'Say it,' I said.

'I'm sorry I ran in front of your car, sir.'

My heart leapt into my chest at the note of sarcasm that Sexto had snuck into his apology, fearing the reigniting of the confrontation. But the cholo hadn't seemed to notice, and instead swaggered back to his car and drove off. We watched as he disappeared into the distance, then I sat next to Sexto on the sidewalk.

'That was very stupid, my friend,' I said.

'Which part?' Sexto responded, letting out a humourless giggle.

'All of it, starting with what happened back at your place.'

Sexto tried to get to his feet, but sat back down, wincing at the pain. Pulling up his shirt, I found a large bruise forming where the beer bottle had hit him. He cried out and drew away from me when I touched the area, pulling back down his shirt.

'You should see a doctor about that in the morning,' I said. 'Just in case.'

'Nah, I'll be all right,' he said in a low voice.

After a moment, I stood and helped him to his feet, and we walked back to his house, neither one of us saying a word. We lingered a bit on his front porch in silence and smoked a cigarette or two, then I gave him a quick hug before turning to leave.

'Why did he call me that?' he blurted out as I descended his front steps.

I looked back at him and saw anxiety etched on his forehead and in the corners of his mouth.

'He called me a faggot. Why did he say that? He doesn't even know me.'

'Don't pay any attention to him,' I said. 'The guy has problems.'

'I have problems, too,' Sexto said. 'But I don't go around calling people names like that.'

'Just forget it, Sexto. Don't let it bother you. It's not worth it.' I climbed the steps and gave his arm a reassuring squeeze, and he nodded, flashing a sad smile before slipping back into his house.

9

Shaitan

I got off the bus at Hillcrest, a few blocks from the Beverly Hills Hotel, where I was supposed to meet Beatrice and Anne to discuss Anne's article about me. Beatrice had offered to send a car, but I preferred to get there on my own. It was noon and sweltering, and I didn't want to soak through the dress shirt and blazer Beatrice had requested me to wear. So I took my time strolling to the hotel along Sunset Boulevard past the massive Beverly Hills mansions built by old-time movie stars like Douglas Fairbanks and Mary Pickford now owned by Arab billionaires.

When I finally arrived at the hotel, a pink Mediterranean-style building perched on a small hill above Sunset Boulevard and nestled in a forest of palm trees and pink bougainvillea, I was fifteen minutes late and starving. The valets and door staff ignored me as I sped past them through the green-and-white striped covered carport and stepped into the grand lobby. It looked like something out of Fantasy Island, plush green carpets, pink walls, pink velour love seats.

A flirty guy with close-cropped red hair and a pug nose, standing behind the concierge desk, pointed the way to the Polo Lounge and whispered something about the dress code as he turned to attend to one of the hotel guests. At the entrance to the Polo Lounge, a middle-aged man with a French accent, a pencil-thin mustache, a tuxedo, and black patent leather shoes, held me back and located my name on a list, and asked me to wait. A moment later, Beatrice came out and greeted me with a kiss on both cheeks, leaving the scent of something expensive on my skin. She looked splendid in a black satin skirt, white chiffon blouse, and a delicate, violet silk scarf that set off her eyes. Her hair was pulled back into a ponytail she held in place with a black, velvet scrunchie.

'The gentleman should be wearing a tie,' the man in the tuxedo said over his shoulder.

I pulled out a blue-and-white bow tie from the breast pocket of my blazer and clipped it on, flashing a wink at the man as Beatrice led me past him arm-in-arm into the restaurant.

'Sorry I'm late,' I said as we slid into a quiet booth at the back of the room. I glanced at the other people scattered around the restaurant. Most of them looked like Westside media whores, sipping on expensive cocktails and engaged in pretentious conversations about movies and money over plates of food they were ignoring.

'I was afraid you'd changed your mind.' Beatrice snapped her fingers at one of the waiters who was walking past, and I felt a sudden hot flash.

'Where's Anne?'

She held up her hand as the waiter stopped by our table, and she ordered a Bloody Mary for herself and a Coke for me.

'I'll have a beer if you don't mind, thanks,' I said.

Beatrice pulled a tight-lip smile and indicated the waiter with a curt nod. 'Be my guest.'

'One Corona, please,' I said. 'With a slice of lime.'

'I'll need to see the gentleman's ID, please.'

I glanced at Beatrice, who arched an eyebrow at me.

'I can't believe he carded me,' I said as the waiter moved away. 'Nobody cards anyone in our neighborhood.'

'Welcome to civilization.' She'd uttered the condescending words in such a light, friendly tone that they didn't register at first. Then they hit home. I pulled off the tie and leaned across the table.

'Where's Anne?' I repeated.

'Anne couldn't make it, I'm afraid.' Beatrice frowned at my open collar. 'She asked me to reschedule something with you.'

'Oh.'

'But since we already had the booking, I thought it would be a perfect opportunity to get to know you better in a more appropriate environment.'

'I see.' I forced a smile and crossed my arms tightly. 'That's too bad. I was looking forward to seeing her again.'

Beatrice stared at me for a moment, then nodded at the menu in front of me. 'Please feel free to order anything you like. The steaks here are superb.'

I slid out of the booth, smoothening out my slacks and buttoning my blazer.

'I need to wash my hands,' I said in answer to her raised eyebrows. 'Which way's the...?'

Beatrice pointed in the direction of the lobby.

As I passed the man at the door, I asked him how many more people were expected to complete our party. He glanced at his list and answered that the reservation was for two people only. When I insisted the table had been booked for a party of three, he checked again, with an air of studied patience, and confirmed it was for two — only two — before turning away.

Beatrice was sipping her Bloody Mary when I returned a few minutes later, a celery stalk forlorn on a side plate. Her eyes tracked me as I approached and slipped back into the booth.

'Everything all right?' she asked.

'Starving, actually.' I reached for a piece of seeded bread from a basket on the table.

The waiter returned as the words came out of my mouth. Beatrice ordered the Lobster Niçoise, and I ordered a tortilla soup and the roasted vegetables. Then we stared at each other across the table for a beat.

'I understand you asked the maître d' about the reservation,' she said.

'If you wanted to ask me out, you didn't have to buy all my paintings and lure me to the Polo Lounge.'

Beatrice's eyes lit up and a ringing laugh escaped her mouth, causing the other patrons to glance in our direction. When she finally recovered herself, she took a sip of water and dabbed at her lips.

'Oh, please, Virgilio. I realize you may consider yourself God's gift to the world, what with your gymnast's body and sacred moniker. But you're much too young for me.' She leaned forward. 'My interest is purely professional.'

'Then what's with the phony meeting with Anne?'

'I'm sorry about that. We're still vetting you before we proceed. I was hoping you and I might be able to chat a bit more about your background. And I wanted to get some additional information about the paintings I purchased, some personal insight from the artist into the subjects. Once I'm satisfied, I'll give the green light to Anne, and we'll schedule the interview.'

I let her words wash over me, working hard to keep my face devoid of all expression. After a moment, she cocked her head, as if she wondered whether I'd heard anything she'd said. I took a sip of my Coke and nodded.

'I'll tell you what,' I said. 'As long as I get to do my own vetting of you, feel free to ask me anything you want.'

'You want to vet me?'

'Yep. For every question you ask me, I get to ask you one. Tit for tat. Total honesty; no secrets.'

The waiter returned, placed our food on the table, and withdrew.

Beatrice was staring at me. I could see her mind working behind those lovely eyes of hers.

'I'll even throw a portrait of you into the deal, barrio style. I'll call it *La Enojada*,' I said, raising my eyebrows at her. 'It means the angry woman.'

'Does it?' A light laugh escaped her lips as she relaxed a bit.

I raised my glass. 'Do we have a deal?'

'We'll see,' she said, clinking her glass against mine. 'Bon appétit.'

After lunch, we went for a walk on the hotel grounds and sat on a pair of lounge chairs on one of the manicured lawns. There was a touch of humidity in the air coming off the lush foliage. A squadron of turquoise dragonflies hummed past on their way to a gurgling fountain a few yards away. I pulled the sketchbook out of my backpack and held it in my lap, trying to decide whether to capture any aspect of the scene laid out before me.

'May I see?' Beatrice asked.

I handed her the pad, and she flipped through it slowly. She stopped at the series of drawings of the crowd at the cockfight.

'What's this?' she asked.

'It's a study for a painting I'm planning.'

She narrowed her eyes at one of the drawings. 'It's very vivid, a bit frightening.' She looked back at me. 'Who are these men?'

'Just a bunch of guys at a kind of sporting event.'

'What kind of sporting event?'

'A fight.'

Beatrice held my gaze. 'I thought the deal was total honesty.'

'All right. It's a scene from a cockfight. They're watching a cockfight.'

'A cockfight? Where, here in Los Angeles? That's illegal, isn't it?'

Now it was my turn to laugh. 'Are you fricking serious? Do you think people in Los Angeles go around doing only legal things? Jeez, you *are* sheltered, aren't you?'

Beatrice suppressed a yawn with the back of her hand. 'Not at all,' she said with a slight air of boredom. 'An artist of your calibre shouldn't be so easily fooled by appearances. I'd expect you could practically see into someone's soul.' She flipped a few pages and handed the pad back to me. She had turned to my sketch of Carino's eyes. 'Like this one.' She traced the forehead with her black-lacquered fingernail. 'What's happening here is nothing less than total despair. It's amazing to me you're able to capture that. Which leaves me wondering whether it was the subject that was feeling it, or if it was you.'

I set aside the sketchpad and turned to her. 'Is that really what bothered you about the cockfight? That it was illegal? What about the animals? You're not concerned about them?'

Beatrice stood and drew a pair of designer sunglasses out of her clutch. 'It's illegal because of the animals.'

'Maybe it's illegal because of the gambling.'

Beatrice lit a long, thin cigarette and took a delicate puff, leaving a lipstick stain on the white paper. 'I let the legislators worry about the ethics. If you'd sketched the cockfight itself, you may have elicited a different reaction from me. But you chose to draw my focus to those horrible men enjoying it, profiting from it. You shouldn't judge me for not reacting to the animal cruelty when it's not even on the page.'

'But that's the thing—' I peered through her sunglasses trying to connect with her eyes. 'It *is* on the page. I showed her the sketch again. 'You can't see it in the bloodhungry expressions?'

Beatrice moved across the lawn in the direction of the building. The conversation was apparently over. I put away my pad and ran to catch up with her.

Twenty minutes later we were standing in a secure, temperature-controlled outbuilding behind her palatial, rose-colored Italianate home in Holmby Hills a couple of miles from the hotel. There were several well-organized shelves containing stacks of paintings in the neutrally painted main room, each carefully numbered and cataloged on a digital system she showed me in a side office.

The five pieces she'd bought at the show were displayed at the far end of the building in an oval-shaped exhibition room furnished with a couple of antique ottomans and wall-to-wall off-white Berber carpet. Each painting sat on its own easel, gently illuminated by a dedicated spotlight. *The Savior of 6th Street* was in the middle with the other four arranged two on each side. Beatrice had draped a cream-colored cardigan over her shoulder when we walked into the air-chilled building. I could see the tips of her nipples poking through her blouse, hard as jawbreakers, and snapped a mental photo of them for later. She indicated the paintings with a sweep of her hand.

'You've interpreted the self-portrait for me. But the others I know nothing about, aside from their titles. I had an idea of getting your interpretation of each of these paintings, one per session, starting with this one.'

She pointed at the piece I called *La Santera*, of a black woman wearing a white tunic and white turban, smoking a cigar, her eyes wide and rolled upward in her head. She was well in the foreground, surrounded by a mad looking crowd in the background, some of them dancing, others on their knees, arms raised heavenward, and above it all a threatening sky, black, red, thunderheads ready to burst over the whole scene.

'That's my mother. She's taking part in a *Santería* ritual. It's a Cuban thing.' My mother's eyes blinked when I mentioned the name of her native religion. They shifted and looked at Beatrice. I held up the palm of my hand at the painting and shook my head.

'This woman's black,' Beatrice said.

'Yep. I'm half black.' I pointed out a young boy in the background, on his knees in front of a fat man clad in white holding a chicken upside down in one hand and a knife in another. 'That's me there.'

Beatrice peered at the painting and looked back at me. My mother's eyes tracked her as she moved; her mouth had turned down into a slight frown. I raised the palm of my hand at her again.

'That's the Santería priest in front of me. He's about to slit a chicken's throat over my head and sprinkle me with blood.'

'I must say, you have a very vivid imagination.'

'This isn't imaginary,' I said. 'It's autobiographical. The imaginative bit comes with how I arrange it all, the colors I use, the apocalyptic sky. But the substance is real. I lived it.'

'Fascinating,' Beatrice said after a few quiet seconds during which she studied the painting. 'Thank you, Virgilio. I think it's enough for now.'

'Do I pass the test?'

Beatrice smiled and turned away. 'Come inside and have some iced tea before you go.'

I walked behind her across the extensive park-like grounds to a side entrance of the main house that led to a restaurant-size kitchen. A cherubic middle-aged Filipina in a traditional cook's uniform — white dress, white cap — poured Beatrice and me two tall glasses of tea over ice with lemon. I followed Beatrice into a flower-filled glass conservatory where we sat across from each other on overstuffed white sofas. Beatrice took a long sip of tea, leaned back against a pillow, and let out a sigh, her eyes closed, a satisfied smile on her face.

I drained my glass in three swallows, feeling a twang in my teeth from the cold liquid, and checked my wristwatch. It was late, and I had to be back in less than two hours for gymnastics at the sports center. As I placed my glass on the coffee table that separated us, the sound of bird's wings flapping and distant cawing came to my ears. It was as if a thousand crows were flying toward us from an eternity away, closer, closer. Then came the smell, a hint of putrefaction, the dead rat you find lodged behind the refrigerator, burst belly seething with new life. I pulled the pad out of my backpack, sketched a single blackbird in flight, and dragged my eraser across its head. The sound stopped, and I was startled by the sound of someone clearing his throat. My heart jumped at the sight of a tall gentleman in his late fifties standing in the doorway dressed in a sharp, tailored brown linen suit, crisp white shirt, hand-painted paisley necktie and shiny burgundy oxfords. His salt-and-pepper hair was cropped close, his eyebrows a pair of fat, black caterpillars, and his dark eyes fierce and intense, which contrasted with his aloof expression. The moment our eyes met, I knew there was going to be trouble.

'Hello, Daddy,' Beatrice said, stretching comfortably on the sofa. She nodded at me. 'This is the artist I was telling you about.'

I stood and extended my hand at the man I'd seen cruising through the tunnels every so often, accompanied by a retinue of bodyguards, inspecting the various side tunnels from which I understood he took a cut of the takings. We all knew him as The King. 'Virgilio Santos, sir.'

The King stepped forward and forcefully shook my hand, nearly pulling me off my feet. 'Maurice Schein. It's a pleasure to meet such a talent.' His voice was resonant, and he spoke with an elegant European accent that was difficult to place, like a cross between French and Italian. He glanced at Beatrice. 'And right here in my own house.' He didn't smile when he said that.

'Virgilio's agreed to be interviewed by Anne,' Beatrice said. 'He's filling me in on each of the paintings I acquired in advance of the interview.'

She rose and looked at my hand, which Schein was still clasping. 'Father was especially drawn to the portrait of the Chinese boy.'

He released my hand, and I rubbed it discreetly against my trousers.

'Aside from the imaginative aspects of your work,' he said, 'you have an uncanny ability to capture the mood of a scene, like Dali at his best. Well done.'

'Thank you, sir.' I wasn't sure whether he recognized me from the tunnels. But the painting of Bruce Lee was a smoking gun, and I feared I wasn't going to be able to escape the bullet.

'I'm hoping to make a *star* out of him, Daddy.' Beatrice drew out the word star in a way that made me feel uncomfortable.

Schein raised an eyebrow at Beatrice just as she'd done at me in the Polo Lounge, then looked at me. 'It seems everyone wants to be a star these days.'

'I'm sorry,' I said, 'but I really have to get going.'

'I'll get you a car,' Beatrice said.

'No, thanks. I prefer to go back on the bus.'

'A bus is not a proper means of travel for a star, young man,' Schein said. 'You'll return home in a car.' He stepped into the hallway, waved at someone, and looked back at me. 'I insist.'

10

Ascencion

The ride home in Schein's black Bentley was surreal. The uniformed driver, a tissue-thin, translucent man of around forty, with soldier-short pale blonde hair, talked incessantly, trying to make conversation with me throughout the ride. He had an annoyingly reedy voice and spoke with a rough-sounding French accent. It turns out he'd worked for Schein for over twenty years and had accompanied him when the family relocated to Los Angeles from Geneva.

'You're originally from Los Angeles?' he asked as we drove slowly east along Sunset in bumper-kissing traffic.

'Yes,' I said, pulling my sketchbook out of my backpack, flipping it open, and burying my head in it.

'And your parents?'

I pretended not to hear him and instead focused on sketching the attractive platinum-haired woman in the car next to us. She was in her late thirties or early forties, dressed in a Denny's waitress uniform, struggling to touch up her lipstick and mascara each time the traffic halted.

The driver twisted his neck and raised his voice. 'Your parents are also from Los Angeles?'

'No,' I said, angling myself toward the window and half-heartedly pencilling in the outline of the woman's lips, which she was pursing and unpursing.

'You like the ladies, eh?' The driver salaciously raised his eyebrows at me in the rearview mirror.

The woman in the other car glanced over at me and smiled. I smiled back and closed my sketchbook, then stuffed it back into my bag and pulled out a book.

'Yeah, sure.' I didn't appreciate the slightly pervy tone the driver was taking with me and was playing with the idea of jumping out of the limo at the next light.

'And Miss Beatrice?'

I snapped shut my book and stared hard at his reflection in his rearview mirror. 'What about her?'

'She's a pretty one, no?' He narrowed his eyes at me and held my gaze for a couple of tense seconds.

'She's a client,' I said between my teeth. 'And you're her father's employee. This isn't exactly an appropriate conversation to be having, is it?'

He looked back at the road and accelerated as he moved to the outside lane in preparation to make a left turn at the intersection with Hollywood Boulevard. 'What do you know of Miss Beatrice's father?'

I stuffed my book into my pack and pressed back against the seat. 'Sorry, man. I'm done.'

'Why is that?' He suddenly applied the brakes, tossing me forward and narrowly avoiding a collision with a Volkswagen bug.

'What the—' I said, sitting up and adjusting my seat belt.

'I apologize for my driving,' he replied and craned his neck to look at me over his shoulder.

I pointed ahead at the traffic, which was moving again. 'You might want to keep your eyes on the road.'

Someone laid on his horn behind us, which made the driver turn around and continue this interminable ride from hell. As we skirted the edge of the Barnsdall Art Park, I focused my attention on the large controlled intersection looming ahead. I prayed to the gods that we'd get held up by a red light, and readied my fingers on the latch to pull open the door.

'I like the ladies, too,' the driver said just as the traffic light at the intersection changed from green to yellow, and he prepared to bring the limo to a stop. 'Especially the dark, passionate ones.' He flashed a wink at me in his rearview mirror.

That was it; I'd had enough of the idiot. The moment the light turned red, I yanked open the door and hopped a southbound RTD that had pulled up to the bus stop next to us and huddled on the opposite side of the bus out of sight of the limo.

As the bus rumbled down Sunset toward Echo Park, the driver's crazy questions kept echoing through my brain, making me dizzy. I rested my head against the cool glass of the window next to my seat and closed my eyes trying my best to regroup. The more I thought about it, the more I suspected he'd been put up to it by either Beatrice or her father. But to what end, in the case of Beatrice? I wondered whether she knew anything about Schein's after-hours activities, whether there was any connection between her enthusiasm for my paintings and his underground business interests, whatever they were. From the way she acted, I thought it likely she didn't know anything. And if that were the case, I imagined Schein wasn't especially keen that she find out, which meant he might consider me a threat if I knew who he was and what he was up to. Either way, the whole thing made me extremely nervous, and I felt lost as to what to do and whom to turn to for advice.

I got out of the bus at Olvera Street, the historic village where the city of Los Angeles began, and strolled across the plaza. The few tourists that were there were browsing Mexican knick-knacks, chewing on *churros*, listening to the roving *mariachi* musicians. As I sped past them, I caught a glimpse of the old mission and changed course. Lowering my head, I stepped across the threshold and entered the chilly darkness of the building. It had been ages since I'd been inside a church. I'd been pretty much faithless since the age of thirteen and only indulged my mother's religious fantasies out of my love and respect for her. But since I knew priests were sworn to silence, I decided to seek advice inside of a confessional booth, feeling like a cliché as I slid the wooden door shut and took a seat, turning the thing over in my mind and waiting for the priest to come along. Ten minutes later I was still waiting.

I started with the premise Beatrice knew about her father's business interests, that she'd seen my work and had recognized the tunnel life I was recording and reported it back to him; that he'd put her up to buying the offending pieces to keep them out of the public eye. If that were the case, as long as I played along, I stood to make some decent money, even though my paintings would never see the inside of a major gallery. But the more I thought about it, the more absurd that scenario seemed. I also considered the opposite: Beatrice knew nothing about her father's secret life as King of the Underworld, and her interest in my paintings was genuine. But now that her father knew about the work, he would want to ensure nobody found out about the source of my inspirations. If this were the case, he'd feel threatened by Beatrice's plans to promote me and would wish to stop her from moving forward. In the end, I considered this the more likely scenario based on their reactions. It was also the more manageable of the two, as I might be able to take control of the situation by pre-emptively seeking out Schein to reassure him of my silence. But if I did that, I'd be complicit with him, which didn't sit well with me. Or, I could just keep clear of the tunnels and paint pretty landscapes.

I stepped out of the confessional and looked around the empty church.

An old Franciscan priest nodded at me as he walked past. I pointed at the confessional. He responded by pointing at a little plaque stating the hours for confession. It seems I'd missed the cutoff for God's afternoon office hours by thirty minutes.

* * *

The lobby of the *Herald Examiner* building was heaving with people rushing in, rushing out. It reminded me of a department store sale the day after Christmas. I asked for Anne Levine at the front desk and ten minutes later she stepped out of one of the elevators, dressed in a man's suit and tie, her black hair pulled back into a ponytail, and looking sexy as all hell. Her face was as impassive as a sphinx.

'I was hoping we might talk,' I said.

She glanced at her watch and nodded at the coffee shop off the lobby.

'Thanks for the write-up about the show,' I said once we were settled at a corner table. 'It really helped boost morale at the center.'

She looked away for a moment, then slowly lowered her cup to the saucer and met my gaze. 'It was an excellent show,' she said woodenly. 'And your work was among my favorites.'

'Thank you,' I said, not quite convinced. 'About that, Beatrice said you wanted to do a feature story about me.'

'Hmmm.' She picked up her cup and took another sip. I noticed she wasn't wearing any lipstick.

'Is that hmmm yes or hmmm what the fuck?'

'Neither. We did talk about it for the fall issue of the arts magazine, and I've pitched the idea to our editor. But nothing's decided yet.'

'I see.' I looked around the coffee shop for a second, leaned across the table and said in a lowered voice, 'Were we supposed to meet at the Polo Lounge this afternoon?'

Anne sat up straight and stared at me for a beat, her thin eyebrows meeting in the middle. 'Why would you ask that?'

'It's a simple question.'

'Certainly not.'

'Were you supposed to meet Beatrice there?'

'I've joined her there before. But nothing recent or in my calendar. What's this about?'

In that instant, I felt something hollow open up in the pit of my stomach. I slid my coffee cup to one side with the back of my hand, and considered what to say next, feeling like a complete idiot. 'Why did she buy my paintings at the show?'

'I told you,' Anne said, angling her body in her chair like she was planning a quick departure from the table, 'we were both taken with your work.'

'Really? Was there any piece in particular that caught her interest?'

'*The Savior of 6th Street* was her favorite, obviously the centerpiece of the collection. Why all the questions?'

'What about the others?'

Anne looked down at the table for a moment, then regarded me over the top of her glasses. 'The one of the Asian boy. That one moved her. But she loved the others as well.' She glanced at her watch and stood. 'I'm sorry, Virgilio, but I'm going to have to rush off.' She put her hand on my shoulder. 'I'll be in touch directly if we decide to do the story.'

I felt like going back to the Westside and confronting Beatrice about the game she was apparently playing with me. But I decided against it and spent the next couple of hours practicing my floor routines at the sports center trying to push it all out of my mind. By the time I was showering, I'd decided it was best to forget any of it had ever happened and hoped she wouldn't come around again. The woman plainly had a problem, and I didn't need any more shit than I already had. Now that her father was in the picture, I thought it best to avoid the tunnels until it all blew over.

That evening at the center, as I started work on a new series of paintings based on my cockfight drawings, Lucinda approached and greeted me with a kiss. She was wrapping up for the day and rushing home to her toddler who her mother was babysitting. I showed her my drawings and explained what I had in mind for the paintings, which I was planning to do in oil on discarded wooden boards, instead of on canvas in my usual acrylic. I wanted to go for a classic look, a twentieth century version of Remy Cogghe's *The Cockfight*. Lucinda loved the idea.

As she was leaving, she turned back and mentioned something about a significant donation she was expecting from an anonymous donor, which often happened right after a show. I congratulated her and tried my best to look happy for her. But I couldn't help thinking Beatrice had something to do with it. I spent the next hour trying to make a start on the painting but was struggling to clear my mind of everything that had gone on that day. So I broke down my easel and stored away my things.

'Beer?' Sexto called out as I sped to the exit.

I spun around and saw him standing alone in the middle of the room. He was smiling, but it was more of a painted smile on a sad-faced clown.

'Hey!' I said, waving him over and giving him a hug.

I'd planned on looking in on Concha, but I hadn't promised her anything. And I needed a break from her drama. So instead I popped out with Sexto into the sultry evening, the heat of the day still radiating off the asphalt, and we headed for my bridge. We spent a couple of hours huddled together on the ledge, sucking on cans of Budweiser I'd scored from the liquor store on the corner where I worked weekends. Two six-packs for a fiver. What a deal. Neither of us was legal to drink, but who the fuck cared? We made our own law in that part of the city.

Sexto chattered on and on about one of the artists from the center he had a crush on, an eighteen-year-old *jeva* from Maywood who called herself La Plumera. She was short and top-heavy, with a cute face she spoiled with plastered-on makeup, dark eyeshadow, and black lipstick.

But, man, could that chick paint. Beautiful portraits of old people in traditional clothes from the countryside of her native *Jalisco*; East LA street scenes that put a lump in my throat. According to Sexto, it was only a matter of time before La Plumera would agree to go out with him.

I fired up a joint once we'd finished the first six-pack, stretched out on my back, and took a hit. Then I handed it to Sexto and closed my eyes. A moment later, I released the smoke and relaxed into the buzz I was feeling from the beer and the pot. I looked up at Sexto, who was staring at the sky, a silly grin breaking out on his face. He looked genuinely happy.

'Are you going down there tonight?' Sexto asked, handing me the joint.

'I don't think so. How about you?'

'I was thinking about it.'

'Molly's again?'

'Feeling super horny. So, yeah, maybe.'

Molly ran a wham-bam operation in one of the side tunnels. She'd set up a half-dozen walk-in-closet-size booths where guys could have a quickie with one of her girls for a twenty. Some nights there was a line that snaked out into the central tunnel.

'Come with me,' he said. 'Maybe Molly will let us split one for a tenner.' He pumped his eyebrows at me.

'Not my thing, '*mano*. But thanks anyway.'

I cracked open another couple cans of beer and handed him one. He set it on the ledge, stepped to one side, and peed over the edge of the bridge, a long stream that went on forever. Then he came back and started in on his next beer.

'What do you know about the King?' I asked him.

'Who?'

'The King, from down there.' I jerked my head in the direction of the tunnels.

'That guy?' Sexto shook his head. 'I don't know anything except he's some mafia dude that runs everything. Why?'

'Just curious. Do you know anything about where he's from or what his day job is?'

'Don't know and don't care. I steer clear of dudes like that. And if you know what's good for you, keep clear of that shit.'

He dug in his pocket and pulled out a little manila envelope the size of a business card, and tapped out a tiny square of white paper with a cartoon of Mickey Mouse in a sorcerer's outfit stamped on it. He held it up to me with a crooked smile.

'Feel like going invisible?'

'I have classes tomorrow.'

'Yeah, in, like, twelve hours. If we do it now, you'll be back to normal when you need to be.'

I shook my head. 'I haven't dropped acid in a long time. Not since that time last year at Arturo's New Year's party. And that didn't go too well for me.'

'Come on, man. It'll be cool. It's all about your headspace. There were too many people at that party, way too distracting for a good trip. Here it's just you and me.'

He waved the little stamp. 'But I've only got one. So we'd have to share.' He scooted up close to me and leaned forward. I could smell the mix of beer and pot on his breath.

'Go for it,' the bridge whispered.

Sexto put the stamp on his tongue. I closed my eyes and felt our mouths merge, lips to lips, tongue to tongue, we French-kissed our way to an acid high, holding each other chest to chest, electricity singing through the wires overhead, intercontinental jets crisscrossing the sky above, our bodies vibrating.

After I don't know how long, ten, twenty, thirty minutes, Sexto pulled me up by the hand, and we gazed out at the viaduct in the direction of

Long Beach. I could see all the way to the coast, past the oil derricks, past the Queen Mary, over the ocean. I could see Hawaii in the distance, Mauna Loa spewing ash and lava and turning the sky red and orange. I looked up and saw a white dove descending. It landed on my shoulder, and the bridge said, 'This is my son.'

The next thing I knew we were floating over the city inside a fat, echoey raindrop, moving down the street, past my apartment block, and humming towards the building works on Alameda. As we drifted down one of the rabbit-hole access points into the tunnels, Sexto kept repeating a load of nonsense about love and respect and about some fantasy he had of the two of us shooting across the sky like Fourth of July fireworks, or something crazy like that. I remember a huge smile plastered on his face that showed off all the gaps between his teeth as he pulled me close and whispered, 'Here's where it all begins.'

Then everything shattered into the seven colors of the rainbow, and I wasn't sure whether I was hearing, seeing, or feeling the red end of the spectrum in the key of E major. But it was warm and soft and cold and hard at the same time, and a rush that started in my chest flowed into the lower half of my body and back again – and again – and I wasn't sure whether I was experiencing the most intense orgasm of my life or a catastrophic loss of blood, which both terrified and excited me to no end. Then everything went black. I felt like I was back in the womb and, at the same time, at rest in my grave, experiencing the entire cycle of life and death in a single, unbroken moment of eternity.

A loud scream brought me back, and I found myself and Sexto racing down a long, narrow tunnel, empty save for a set of iron rails that ran down the middle and a thick, sepia fog that enveloped us. We were screaming at the top of our voices and running at full speed, Sexto on one side of the rails, and me on the other. Somehow I knew we were in a smaller tunnel running parallel to the larger tunnel, one level below, speeding toward Long Beach. What I wasn't sure of was whether we were running from something or toward something. Then the fog cleared, and I heard the sound of heavy footsteps on concrete echoing behind us, gaining on us. Sexto let out a yelp and pulled ahead, his arms pumping hard, his head pivoting from side to side, sprinting like a complete madman. And then he disappeared.

I woke up the next morning, naked in my own bed. My head was throbbing and felt stuffed full of cotton. I reached for the clock on my nightstand to check the time and froze in mid-motion at the sight of a rust-colored feather next to it. I snatched it up in my trembling hand and stared at it, trying hard to remember how I'd gotten home and hoping it would provide some clue. But I couldn't remember anything. My memory was a complete blank. It was 7:50 in the morning, and I had to get going to school. So I shoved the feather into a drawer and rolled out of bed.

After a hot shower, I threw on a pair of jeans and a white T-shirt and headed to the kitchen. I found my mother sitting at the table, sipping her *café con leche*. Across from her was my steaming cup, and in the middle of the table our typical breakfast of Cuban crackers, butter, and guava jam. My mother was still in her waitress uniform. There were dark circles under her eyes, which were droopy and tired-looking. Once I left for school, she'd quickly catch up on her sleep and then head out to the factory where she worked part-time late mornings sewing buttons on shirts. I kissed her on the forehead and sat at the table.

'What did you do last night?' she asked abruptly.

I leaned back and straightened my hair. 'Nothing. Just hung out on the bridge with Sexto, my friend from the center.' I averted my eyes, afraid to mention anything to her about the feather, as she would take it as a bad omen.

My mother set down her cup on the saucer; it clattered as it made hard contact. She leaned forward and pulled my hair away from my forehead.

'Stay out of it please, Mamá. None of your shenanigans.'

'Listen to you with those fancy words.'

'I'm serious, Mamá. I can take care of myself.'

'Hmmm...' She gave a little shrug and leaned back in her chair.

The silence grew heavy as I buttered a cracker and dipped it into my coffee, trying my best to avoid making eye contact with her.

'I don't like that girl,' she said as I raised the dripping cracker to my mouth. 'She's up to no good.'

I dropped the cracker to my plate. 'What girl?'

'You know what girl, smarty pants. The one who lured you to her palace.'

'She didn't lure me anywhere, Mamá. She's just a rich, spoiled lady who thinks she owns the world. But she *did* buy all my paintings. So that counts for something, doesn't it?'

'I don't know.' She shrugged and waved her hand at me. 'Go to school. It's late. I need you home by five this afternoon. Remember, we have *la reunion* tonight.'

11

Babalú-Ayé

I spotted Beatrice from the bus window, sitting in her sports car in the parking lot across the street from my apartment block. She was wearing a dark blue scarf over her hair and a pair of round sunglasses and had the sun visor pulled down. Rather than get off at the stop in front of where she was parked, I got off at the next one, right before the bridge, walked the few blocks back, and approached her car from behind. She almost jumped out of her seat when I knocked on the driver's side window.

'Jeez Louise,' she said, lowering the window, 'you scared me half to death.'

'Hello, Beatrice.'

She got out of the car and leaned against the door, pushing her sunglasses up on her head.

'I called the center. Someone there told me you take classes at LACC and usually get home around this time.' She nodded in the direction of my apartment across the street. 'I pressed the buzzer, but nobody was home. So I decided to wait.'

'What are you doing here?'

'Can we go somewhere to talk?'

'You lied to me,' I said. 'Anne didn't know anything about the meeting at the Polo Lounge. And she hasn't decided about interviewing me.'

'I'm sorry about that,' she said. 'I'll explain it all, I promise. But, I have to talk to you about something else.'

I glanced at my watch. My mother would be home in about an hour.

'Follow me,' I said, moving to the sidewalk, 'we can talk at my place.'

Beatrice slinked into my darkened apartment and her mouth drooped open as she glanced around at the statues and paintings of the various saints. Her gaze settled on the fruit-laden altar with its flickering votive candles, and she drifted toward it. I shut the door loudly and crossed the room to raise the blinds to let in some outside light. When I turned around, she was still staring at the altar.

'Earth to Beatrice Schein,' I called out, setting my book bag on the kitchen table and sitting side-saddle in one of the chairs.

Beatrice tore her gaze away from the altar. 'This is fascinating,' she whispered, methodically casting about, examining every detail of the tiny apartment. 'I've never seen anything quite like this.'

'What did you want to talk about?'

Beatrice blinked and looked at me, as if noticing me for the first time, her face becoming serious. She crept across the room, pulled out a chair at the table opposite me, and leaned in.

'I had a dream last night,' she said in a low voice, quickly glancing over her shoulder. 'That black woman from your painting.'

'My mother?'

Beatrice nodded.

'I saw her in a dream. She was staring at me. I tried to get away, but no matter where I went, she was there, just staring at me with these really wide eyes.'

'It doesn't surprise me,' I said. 'You and I were talking about her yesterday. She was bound to stick in your mind.'

'No. It was more than that; not like any dream I've ever had before,'

Beatrice said. 'It was almost as if she were actually inside my head. And when I woke up, there was this instant when I felt she was in my room, watching me from the foot of my bed, dressed like she was in the painting, all in white.'

'You were probably still half asleep.'

Beatrice opened her purse, pulled out a folded piece of white linen, and put it on the table.

'What's that?' I asked.

'It's my pillowcase. Smell it.'

I unfolded the pillowcase and put it to my nose. It stank of cigar smoke.

'Nobody smokes in my home,' Beatrice said.

I folded the pillowcase and pushed it back at her across the table.

'I don't know what to say.'

Beatrice slipped the pillowcase back into her purse and shook her head.

'Now, if you don't mind, I'd like some answers,' I said. 'What's this game you're playing with me?'

'It's a long story,' Beatrice said, her voice dropping to a whisper.

'Oh my God,' I said, standing and grabbing a pitcher of water out of the refrigerator. 'Please don't insult my intelligence with a stupid platitude.'

She went on as if she hadn't heard me. 'I spent my last year of high school in Cape Town, in South Africa, with an aunt — my father's sister — and her family. My parents were having problems that year, and I was a bit of a handful, always yearning for adventure. So we all agreed it was best for everyone if I went. When I was there, I met Teko, a black boy from one of the townships. He was working as a cook at a neighbor's house.' Beatrice took a sip of water and drew a long breath, looking both vulnerable and defiant. 'We ran away together.'

I pulled out my sketchpad and opened it to a blank page, my pencil poised over it. Beatrice glanced at me then averted her eyes. I started with an outline of her face.

'You reminded me of Teko,' she continued, 'the afternoon we met. There was something about your manner, your voice; I don't know. Then there was that painting, the self-portrait. The expression on the face of the Savior figure.' She looked directly at me. 'It was Teko. It's why I bought the painting.'

I set aside the pad. 'I still don't get it. Why did you have to pretend about the rest?'

'It's not a pretense. I couldn't just buy your self-portrait without raising the suspicions of my parents, especially my father. He didn't exactly approve of my relationship with Teko. So, instead, I bought all your paintings and made it more about you as an artist.'

'I see.'

'Don't get me wrong, Virgilio. I sincerely believe you're a great artist. And I fully intend to do everything in my power to promote you. But I first want to make sure I know as much about you as possible before committing myself to the project.'

'What happened with Teko?'

Beatrice shook her head and closed her eyes.

Suddenly the door to our apartment flew open, and a current of air from the stairwell sent the papers in the room all aflutter. We both looked up, and a moment later my mother appeared in the doorway, a shopping bag in her arms. I ran to the door and took the shopping bag from her and put it in the kitchen. When I turned around I found my mother and Beatrice staring at each other, my mother's head cocked to one side, her widening eyes glowing in the dim light of the room, her pupils expanded to the edges of her mocha-colored irises. Beatrice was standing across from her, clutching the strap of her purse as if for dear life.

'Beatrice, this is my mother Celia Santos; Mamá, this is Beatrice

Schein, the woman who bought my paintings.'

'I know who she is.' My mother stepped around Beatrice, never taking her eyes off her, examining her as if measuring her for a shroud. 'She's a beautiful girl.'

Beatrice shot a look at me, and I shrugged.

'I'll walk you to your car,' I said to Beatrice.

'Where are you going?' my mother snapped.

'I'll be right back,' I said, 'I'm just seeing her out.'

'I meant her.' My mother lifted her chin at Beatrice.

'She's going now, Mamá. We have to leave for the meeting in a few minutes.'

'She can come along.'

* * *

When we arrived at the basement apartment in Echo Park, la reunion was in full swing. A faint echo of drumming filled the stairwell as we entered the building. It increased in volume as we descended into the bowels of the building and knocked us back when the apartment door flew open in response to my mother's series of sharp raps with her stone encrusted walking stick.

Beatrice followed my mother inside, with me trailing behind. My mother was wearing a flowing white dress and a white turban decorated with three bright red flowers, and an assortment of multicolored necklaces. I'd changed into a pair of white trousers, a white shirt, and a white cap. The door slammed shut behind us as we moved down a candle-lit passage toward the cramped, windowless room in the back of the apartment where the ceremony was taking place. Beatrice glanced over her shoulder at the door and narrowed her eyes at me, and I applied a little pressure to her shoulder to keep her moving forward.

A dozen devotees filled the room, maybe more, sitting on chairs in a semicircle, most of them dressed in white, chanting and swaying to the sounds of rhythmic drumming. They were a mix of women and men of all ages, from shriveled old ladies in their nineties to lanky adolescents, black, white, and everything in between. They faced a multitiered altar across a narrow, open space at the far end of the room, partially hidden behind a transparent, lace-edged piece of fabric pinned to the ceiling that served as a curtain. The usual trinity of saints topped the altar: San Lazaro; the Virgen del Cobre; and, my favorite, the ever-present Santa Barbara – Changó in drag. Surrounding the saints and filling each level of the altar were offerings of tropical fruit, burning candles, water-filled jars stuffed with cigars, and scores of rosaries. The moment my mother appeared, the crowd greeted her as if she were an A-list celebrity, hugging and kissing her. She pulled a hand-painted fan from her bag and used it to point out a corner for Beatrice and me to occupy, then she sat with three other women dressed almost identically to her.

Beatrice's face was a study in impassivity. She studied the crowd with shifting eyes, hardly moving her head, but never once did her face take on the slightest expression, not interest, not delight, and certainly not fear. Her feet didn't move with the infectious rhythms from the various drummers scattered around the room. Even when the chanting, which was just a murmur when we first arrived, began to increase, becoming progressively louder with each round of the drumming, and the swaying of the group erupted here and there into spontaneous dancing, Beatrice held steady and stared straight ahead.

It was only when my mother stood and pulled out a cigar, which one of the other women lit for her, did I notice Beatrice blink. Her head turned somewhat in the direction of my mother, and I caught sight of the slightest trembling of her lip. A scream rang out over the group as my mother raised her hands to the ceiling, and the music stopped. Complete silence descended over the room, save for the cackling of a couple of chickens in a crate on the floor next to the altar. My mother strode forward, drew in a deep drag from her cigar, and zigzagged the room, blowing smoke over the crowd. When she was opposite us, she opened her eyes wide at Beatrice and clapped her hands three times, and the drumming started again. Beatrice took in a sharp breath. I touched her arm, giving it a quick squeeze of reassurance, though I had felt the threat as much as she did. Catching sight of my hand, my mother spun away from us and moved back into the middle of the room, where she danced the ritual dance for the saints.

'It was her,' Beatrice whispered to me.

I looked at her.

'Last night in my dream, it was your mother. I don't know how or why, but she was right there in my bedroom.'

'We can go if you like.'

She shook her head. 'I want to see the rest.'

A slender mulatta of around forty, barefoot and wearing a red housedress, rose from her chair and started dancing in front of my mother, her eyes closed, her face ecstatic. She chanted and swayed, her dancing becoming jerky and erratic, then she fell to the ground and screamed words nobody in that room understood, except for my mother and the Santería priest that appeared from out of nowhere. Everyone rose to their feet and surrounded the woman, who flailed and shouted and foamed at the mouth. The drumming stopped. After a moment, the woman's screaming subsided, and she fell into a deep trance. My mother and the priest interpreted the woman's words to the crowd; it was a message from the orisha that had possessed her, words of encouragement, words of warning.

'Had enough?' I asked Beatrice as the crowd returned to their chairs and started the low chanting again.

'What's happening now?' she asked, nodding at a small group of people lining up in front of the priest, a grizzled man in his early forties with a heavily pockmarked face, dressed in white and wearing a red bandana. He pulled one of the chickens out of the crate, and the people kneeled and bowed their heads.

'Oh shit.'

'This is exactly like in your painting,' she said.

'You might want to avert your eyes right about now,' I said.

Beatrice moved away from me, stepped to the side of the crowd, and didn't flinch when the priest slit the chicken's throat and sprinkled blood and chanted a blessing over the heads of each person kneeling in front of him. My mother sidled over and looked me in the eye.

'Be very careful with that one, hijo,' she whispered. 'She's dark inside. Las Otras sense it too.'

I glanced at Las Otras, the three Santeras my mother was sitting with. They nodded at me and directed their gaze at Beatrice who was now on her knees in front of the priest, her head lowered, receiving his blessing, a dead chicken hanging limply in his arms.

12

Tentacles

A tap on my shoulder pulled me out of the zone. I turned away from the cockfight painting I was working on and found Concha standing behind me dressed in skin-tight blue jeans, white tennis shoes, and a plain white blouse. Her hair was pulled away from her face and held in place with a simple rubber band. She wriggled her fingers at me in a shy greeting, then bounded forward and kissed me on the cheek.

'Whatcha working on, sweetie?' she said, stepping up to the painting.

I looked at the three other artists in the studio focused on their paintings and back at Concha who was pursing and unpursing her lips.

'Recognize it?' I asked.

She stepped back and looked me straight in the eye.

'Maybe you shouldn't be painting that.' The corners of her mouth turned down. 'Or at least change it up the way you do.'

'Why?'

She glanced at the painting and back at me. 'I recognize a couple of those guys. It's not cool. People might get mad.'

'Not working tonight?'

'Don't go changing the subject on me, smart-ass. I'm serious.'

'So am I.'

Concha shook her head and glanced around the room, looking a bit lost.

'How about if we take that ride to the beach tonight, just like you wanted?' she said.

I checked my watch. 'I've been blowing off my work too much lately, Concha. Come back in an hour.'

I broke down my things at nine o'clock and put them in the locker and shared a quick beer on the patio with a couple of the other guys before popping outside to look for Concha. It was so foggy I couldn't see more than a block in either direction. In the distance, I could hear the echo of cars on the freeway. But 1st Street was deserted.

I pulled on my hoodie and waited around ten minutes, leaning against the building in the glow of the yellow safety light, when I caught sight of Sexto limping down the hill toward me from the direction of Boyle Heights, a wide grin on his face. He was dressed in knee-length chinos, long white socks, a white T-shirt, and a black watch cap.

'What happened to *you*, bad boy?' I asked.

Sexto grabbed my hand and pulled me into a hug.

'That fall fucked me up, vato,' he said, beaming a big smile. 'It got me ten stitches on my leg and twisted something in my ankle.'

A vague recollection of a fall in a dark place and some screaming came to me from the other night when we were tripping.

'You don't remember anything, do you, *carnal*?'

I shook my head. 'Not much.'

'We went underground that night. We thought the acid made us invisible, remember? So we went down there and shared that redhead at Molly's.'

'I don't remember that.'

'Dude, you were really going at it, it was so hot. I still get hard just thinking about how you looked while you were pumping that jeva. It was like watching live porn.'

'Fuck, man. My mind's a complete blank.'

'Later we got lost in the dark and somehow ended up in that other tunnel, the secret one, where some of those dudes who work for the King chased us halfway to Long Beach, and I fell off a ledge. After that, the big man himself showed up and had a couple of them take me to County General.' Sexto fished a wad of cash out of the pocket of his chinos and pushed it at me. 'They gave me this and told me to keep quiet.'

My mouth went dry at the mention of the big man.

Sexto stuffed the cash back in his pocket and handed me a black bandana. 'Wipe your face, carnal. You're sweating like a *puerquito*.'

'How is it your memory's so good when I can't remember a thing?' I passed the bandana over my face and handed it back to him.

Sexto shrugged. 'I'm not a lightweight like you. Anyway, the big man asked where you live so he could get you home.'

'You shouldn't have told him, Sexto.'

'I didn't! I might be brown, but I ain't stupid. I just kept moaning like I didn't hear what they were saying, then they took me out of there.'

'So how did I get home?'

'Hell if I know.'

'I woke up in my bed, man. Naked under the covers. With my memory wiped.'

'Like I said, I don't know. Maybe you just made it home on your own.'

He raised his head at the downtown. I turned and saw Concha strolling up the hill in our direction now wearing a royal blue knit pullover. I looked back at Sexto.

'Did he say anything else? The big man?'

'Like what?'

'Like anything.'

Sexto shook his head. 'Nah, nothing, man. Hey, Concha.'

Concha planted a kiss on Sexto's cheek, and he slid his face around to kiss her on the mouth. Concha let out a throaty little scream and fake-slapped him across the face. 'Don't get fresh, you.' She put her arms around my neck and rested her head on my shoulders. I could smell beer on her breath.

'What do you say we go and have ourselves a threesome?' Sexto pumped his eyebrows at me.

Concha lifted her head and stared into my eyes, her eyebrows meeting in the middle. 'What's wrong, mijo? You're, like, all stiff and pale.'

'I'll tell you later. Let's go catch that bus.'

'Where are you two going?' Sexto asked.

I squeezed Concha's hand, hoping she'd get the signal and not mention the beach.

'Loverboy and I have a date,' she said. 'And little boys ain't invited. Sorry.'

Sexto hiked up his chinos. 'This boy ain't little.' He moved up to us and winked at the lower half of his body. 'In fact, he's getting bigger as we speak.'

'I'll pass, *grosero*, thanks.' Concha shook her head at me.

'Suit yourselves,' Sexto said, moving past us and down the hill. 'I'm gonna go find me some trouble.' He disappeared into the fog.

* * *

Concha and I rode next to each other in the back of the all-nighter that ran down Wilshire Boulevard to Santa Monica. She curled up on the seat like a cat and rested her head on my lap. Peering out the window, I was surprised to see how dense the fog had gotten. I couldn't make out anything, and my anxiety was growing at the thought that maybe it wasn't even safe for us to be driving in it. But by the time we reached the city limits of Santa Monica and neared the ocean, it had lifted enough for us to see the lights of the pier in the distance.

Concha and I kicked off our shoes and strolled onto the sand, walking out to where it was damp and bubbly from a receding wave. There was a pungent smell of salt water in the air. Mournful cries of seabirds echoed off the fog every so often. Concha held my hand tight as the cold water glided back onshore and enveloped our feet. She squealed at the first shock of the contact, and I felt a shiver run through her as we waited to get used to the temperature. Then the water receded, and we moved back to the dry sand and dropped onto it.

I glanced up and down the deserted beach and at the pier in the distance. All the lights were turned off. It looked abandoned, save for the furtive movement of some random streeters creeping among the buildings.

'Just like in high school,' Concha said, her first words since we'd left downtown. She stretched out on her back and stared heavenward into the fog.

I kicked my feet out in front of me and leaned back on my hands.

'Yeah,' I said. 'Only we're not in high school anymore, are we?'

Concha closed her eyes.

'Thank fuck for that,' she whispered, a smile breaking out on her face.

'Right, thank fuck.'

Concha opened her eyes and looked at me. 'What's bothering you, mijo?'

I shook my head and stared out at the ocean.

'Is it that rich bitch? Cause if it is, I'll fuck her up.'

The image of Concha and Beatrice fighting made me laugh. I pictured the two of them going at it like a pair of cocks hurling themselves at each other, pecking at each other's eyes, surrounded by a screaming crowd.

'What's funny, mijo? I'm dead serious. I heard she's been hanging around.'

'She came with my mother and me to a reunion in Echo Park.'

Concha sat up. 'What the fuck? How did *that* happen?'

'My mother made her come.'

Concha nodded. She knew my mother.

'I thought she'd run out of there the moment she saw what was going on. But she didn't. She stayed all the way through and accepted a blessing from the *curandero*.'

Concha rolled her eyes. 'That chick's weird.'

A group of about a half-dozen young white guys on bicycles came riding by on the boardwalk screaming nonsense into the night, forcing a lull in the conversation. I waited until the fog had completely swallowed them up, and the only sound left was the lapping of the breakers on the shoreline, before I spoke again, albeit with some reluctance.

'Concha...?'

Concha levelled her heavily made up eyes at me, one side of her mouth pulling up slightly.

'Do you know who the King is?' I asked.

Concha blinked and stayed quiet.

'The King from the tunnels, you know. That tall dude in the dark suit and scarf who cruises around down there with his bodyguards.'

Concha didn't go into the tunnels very often. In fact, I'd only seen her down there a couple of random times on the arm of a date. But she knew everyone, or at least everyone knew her.

'I've heard about him,' she said, the volume of her voice noticeably dropping. She looked away and focused her attention on her toes, wriggling them to clear them of sand. 'But I ain't never actually seen him...'

'What have you heard?'

Concha shrugged and looked back up at me. 'He's some badass people pay to let them run their businesses. I guess.'

'He's Beatrice's father.' I hadn't intended to let the *gato* out of the *saco* yet, but it just came pouring out like I had no control over my mouth. My heart jumped into my chest, and I glanced around. The smell of cigar smoke was in the air. Concha smelled it too, I could tell.

'Oh, mijo—' She touched my shoulder, her face a sudden spasm of anxiety. 'Are you sure?'

'I'm sure. I saw him at her house on the Westside. She took me there to see the paintings she'd bought and introduced him to me. I wasn't sure he recognized me. But then—'

'But then what?'

I recalled what Sexto had told me, about what had happened in the tunnel, and felt a hot-cold current course through my body.

'I don't know. He might have seen me down there afterward.'

'Be careful, mijo. Steer clear of that shit. And don't go painting any more of what goes on down there. That dude's a mean fuck. You don't want to piss him off. Stick to portraits and street scenes.'

'I thought you didn't know him.'

'I don't.'

'You just said he's a mean fuck. How do you know?'

'I was just saying, obviously.'

'Concha.'

She pulled back and looked away.

'He's one of your guys, isn't he?'

Concha stood and slapped the sand off the back of her jeans.

'Just keep clear of that shit,' she repeated. 'And stay away from her too.'

I stood and stared at Concha, who was doing her best to avoid making eye contact with me. I knew better than to pump her for information once she shut down. But her reaction told me enough. She knew the King. Probably too well.

I walked to the edge of the water and stared into the distant dark, fighting back the sadness welling up inside. I couldn't trust Concha anymore. She'd been my best friend for years. And now she was making herself a stranger to me.

She came up from behind. Her sandy fingers intertwined with mine. She tried to rest her head against my arm, but I shifted away, still holding her hand.

'You know what?' Her voice was quiet, almost a whisper.

'What?'

'We should get married and move away from here. We can go somewhere exciting like Acapulco and start over.'

'Sounds nice.'

I let go of her hand and trudged across the sand, snatching up my shoes as I passed where we'd been sitting, and perched on the edge of the boardwalk to empty them of sand and slip them back on. Concha stayed at the water's edge.

13

Teko

Anne and I sat next to each other having coffee on the patio of the art center, wrapping up her recently approved interview with me. It had been an intense few hours, escorting her around my neighborhood and the art center, answering her questions about my background, my inspirations, my methods. This last stop was a breather before her final series of questions.

She alternated between checking her notes and sipping her coffee. The late afternoon sunlight made her honey-colored skin glow, enhancing the contrast with her hazel eyes and raven hair. After a few minutes, she closed her steno pad and regarded me over her glasses.

'This has been surprisingly productive.' She flashed one of those big Anne Levine smiles I remembered from the day I met her. 'Thanks very much for letting me into your world and for being forthcoming with your answers. I'd understood from Beatrice you might be somewhat reticent.'

'She's right,' I said, draining the last of my coffee. 'I'm a private person. I prefer for people to get to know me through my paintings. But something like this doesn't come around very often. So I was okay with making an exception.'

I gave a thumbs-up to Lucinda who had pulled back the curtain of her office to check on us. Anne pivoted around and raised her hand in a little wave.

'She's lovely,' she said.

'She's a damned good administrator. And not a bad sculptor as well, when she has the time.'

'Is that so?'

'Those two pieces in the reception room are hers.'

Anne closed her eyes, remembering. 'You mean those so-high pillars on either side of the door that look like totem poles?

'Bingo. She made them of found stuff.'

Anne nodded. 'Nice, but not the kind of sculpture I had in mind. Reminds me in a strange way of the Watts Towers, which are one of a kind, but not something that grabs my attention, if I'm honest.'

I nodded and looked to one side feeling a sudden dip in my emotions. Her mention of the Watts Towers took me by surprise and brought back black memories of the last time I'd seen my father.

'I suppose my last question is, what are your plans for the future? Where do you see Virgilio in five years?'

I looked back at her, her eyebrows raised expectantly, the moisture still on her lips from her last sip of coffee, and felt a tug inside, a flicker of desire. I found myself imagining the two of us in bed, her legs wrapped around my back as I moved in and out of her, my face buried in her neck, her fingers interlacing my hair and tugging tighter the closer she got to orgasm. Just then, a couple of artists burst into the patio followed by Sexto, dispelling the fantasy. They struggled across the courtyard, hefting an antique sideboard between the three of them, using the patio as a shortcut to the other side of the center. Sexto winked at us as they passed. A moment later they disappeared through another door, leaving us alone again.

Anne blinked at the door and looked back at me.

'Sorry about that,' I said. 'This is meant to be the quietest place here.'

Anne shook her head. 'I was asking about your plans.'

'Right,' I said. 'As I said before, I'm studying at LACC, Fine Arts and English Literature. After that, I might want to get a master's, maybe at some place like UCLA; I don't know. We'll see.'

'And after that?'

'Don't know. Maybe I'll teach or something. In the meantime, I'll just keep doing what I'm doing. Sketching, painting, exhibiting. I'm not that ambitious.'

'No?'

'I'm pretty happy with my life.'

'No hopes for fame and riches?'

'Nope. I don't even play the lottery.'

'Wife, kids, a house in the suburbs with a white picket fence and a dog?'

I shook my head. 'Just me and my mother, living in our little apartment until someone comes along and tears it down. After that, who knows? For now, you know where to find me for the next few years.'

Anne stood and stretched her legs. The interview was over.

'I don't know whether to admire you or—'

'Or what?'

Anne shrugged and shouldered her purse. 'I find your lack of ambition a bit odd. I don't know whether to believe you or not.'

She suddenly looked less attractive to me.

'What about you?' I asked. 'Where do you see yourself in five years?'

'I thought I was asking the questions.'

'The interview's over now, isn't it?'

Anne glanced at her watch. 'Yes, it is.'

'So we're on my time now.'

Anne arched an eyebrow at me.

'What's your five-year plan, Anne? Editor at the *Herald*? House in Malibu? Husband, kids, holidays in Europe? Visiting the Taj Mahal? Climbing Mount Everest?'

'All of the above, I would hope,' she said with a half smile.

I lowered my voice and stepped up to her. 'And what if you don't get any of it? What if in five years you're still stuck behind a junior editor's desk interviewing nobodies like me, living in the same two-bedroom apartment in wherever you live, still hoping to meet Mr. Right? What then?'

Anne stared at me for a moment, shook her head and started toward the door. I followed her to her car, a black, late-model Ford Taurus with a thin layer of dust adhering to the body. There was a scratch on the passenger's side door as if someone had keyed it recently. It was already dark outside.

'The article should be out in next month's issue,' she said, shaking my hand. Hers felt cold. 'I'll have the office mail a couple of copies here to the center to your attention.'

'Sorry about that over there.' I glanced in the direction of the center. 'Don't know what got into me.'

Anne nodded. 'It's been a long, emotion-filled day. I understand.'

'Maybe we could see each other again sometime.' I touched her shoulder and flashed an apologetic smile. 'Let me make it up to you.'

'That's really not necessary.'

'We could catch that drink...and see where things go from there.'

Anne looked me straight in the eye for a moment, then pulled out her keys. 'Be careful what you wish for.'

No sooner had she driven off than Sexto stuck his head out of the center and yelled for me about an urgent phone call. It was Beatrice, eager to know how things had gone. She invited me out that night for, as she put it, a celebratory dinner at one of her favorite restaurants. I had just enough time to get home and change into something decent before she was pressing the buzzer to my apartment. I could tell from her subdued manner she'd already spoken to Anne.

She greeted me with a kiss on both cheeks and congratulated me on the interview; she even smiled a bit. I still remember how angelic she looked standing outside our building in her white dress illuminated by the glow of the street lamp. She'd lifted her head at the sound of drilling in the distance; the construction workers had just started their work for the night.

'Welcome to our nightmare.' I'd nodded at the glaring lights a block away.

'What is that?'

'They're building the subway.'

Beatrice had crinkled her nose and shook her head. 'It's quite loud.'

'When they get all four drilling machines going, it's like standing on an airport tarmac. Some people can't sleep for the noise. We're talking six days a week.'

We ended up at a quiet French restaurant in Los Feliz not far from the Greek Theatre where the maître d' gave us a booth in the back with a privacy curtain. A bottle of champagne was chilling in an ice-filled bucket next to our table when we arrived after an uncomfortable ride in Beatrice's sports car during which she'd uttered only a few words.

Once the cork was popped and the champagne poured, Beatrice's mood seemed to lighten. We raised our glasses, and she proposed a toast to my success and — she paused — to the future, emphasizing the word with an extra nod of her head, looking straight into my eyes as our glasses clinked together. We took a sip or two and sat quietly for a couple of awkward seconds.

'It really *is* bright, you know,' she said. 'If you allow it to be.'

'What is?'

'Your future.'

I nodded and took another sip of champagne. 'What did she tell you?'

'That you reacted badly when she asked you about your plans.'

I pasted a tight smile on my face.

'There's nothing wrong with having plans,' she said. 'The world couldn't get on without plans. I mean, you can't possibly want to live where you do for the rest of your life in that cramped apartment in one of the most economically depressed neighborhoods in the entire city.'

'To set the record straight, it wasn't her question about my plans that set me off. It was something she said about the Watts Towers. She was comparing a couple of Lucinda's sculptures to them.'

Beatrice set down her glass. 'What about them?'

'My father lives right across from them. Or at least he did the last time I saw him almost four years ago now.'

'You haven't seen your father in four years?' There was something annoyingly self-righteous about the way she'd said the words.

We were interrupted by the waiter who pulled back the curtain to our booth and brought us our first course. It seemed Beatrice had pre-ordered everything, our meal, the wine, the bottles of both still and sparkling water. Once he withdrew, Beatrice repeated her question.

'Like I told you before, he abandoned us when I was four. My mother came home one day, and he was gone, clothes and everything. No goodbye note, nothing. She was so upset, she destroyed all her pictures of him except for one she saved for me so I could know what he looked like.'

'How awful.'

'For her, yeah. It wasn't so bad for me at first since I was little at the time. The truth is I didn't even remember him. But as I got older, I did wonder where he'd got off to. We heard rumors he'd gone back to Mexico, some neighbor of ours said she thought he might have died in an accident, someone else speculated he had another family somewhere. I tried not to let it bother me too much. But it was always there in the back of my head, this feeling of having been dumped.'

Beatrice watched me quietly as I tore off a piece of bread and tucked into a shallow bowl of soup, which was already growing cold. We both finished our soups and set them aside to wait for the next course.

'You said you saw him four years ago.'

'Yeah, I was working in a liquor store on the corner near where you park across from our apartment. I'd just turned sixteen. Some lady came into the store and started chatting with me. Turns out she was a cousin of his. She told me where he worked in South Central less than ten miles from us. A straight shot down Central Avenue. So I went to see him.'

'How did that go?'

'He owned this little electronics repair shop at Compton and 108th in a dilapidated strip mall. I walked in and introduced myself. The asshole acted as if he'd seen me the day before.'

'Maybe his cousin told him you were coming.'

'Maybe. But I didn't expect that nothing reaction. I mean, for God's sake, here's the son you abandoned twelve years ago. You have no idea whether he's there to hug you or kill you. And you treat him like he's some fucking customer that walked in off the street. Sorry for my language.'

'You're still angry.'

'I'm not angry. I just expected more from him. I was disappointed and upset because I'd been building up the whole thing in my mind. But I didn't let him see it. I just sat there waiting two hours for him to close up and followed him home. He was living alone a five-minute walk from his shop in a crumbling backyard bungalow right across the street from the Watts Towers, that pile of junk. He served me coffee in his living room and sat there like a dummy.'

'Did you ask him why he left?'

'Yeah.'

'And?'

'He blamed it on my mother. Said he couldn't handle her. He claimed she sent him away. Something about her putting a hex on him. I don't know; maybe she did. After I left there, I went home and burned his picture and never went back.'

Beatrice put her hand on my wrist.

I pulled back my arm. 'I only told you about that because of the Anne thing. When she mentioned the Watts Towers, it reminded me of him, and the rest went downhill from there. You can explain it to her next time you talk to her.'

We ate the rest of our dinner in silence. I noticed Beatrice dabbing at her eyes with her napkin every so often.

'I'm sorry,' I said as we were picking at the last of our dessert. 'I didn't mean to upset you.'

Beatrice shook her head. 'Not at all. I'm the one who should be apologizing. This was supposed to be a celebration. But that story you told about your father, it reminded me so much about Teko, that boy I spoke to you about.'

'The one you ran away with?'

Beatrice looked off to the side and narrowed her eyes as if conjuring up an image. After a moment she nodded and looked back at me.

'His father abandoned him as well. It deeply affected him. He found it difficult to trust anyone because of that.'

'What happened to him?'

Beatrice's eyes filled with tears again, and she dried them with her napkin. Then she excused herself and left the table. I sat there for a while, waiting for her to come back. When, after a few minutes, she still hadn't returned, I pulled back the curtain and looked across the dining room. It was nearly empty, save for a waiter gliding across the room and a handful of diners chatting over the last of their coffees. I slid out from the table and asked the maître d' if he'd seen Beatrice. He indicated the entrance of the restaurant with a nod of his head.

I found Beatrice standing outside, smoking a cigarette. She was gazing up at the moon, a serene smile on her face. In the distance, I could make out the music from a concert at the open-air Greek Theatre.

'Are we done?' I asked.

She turned around and smiled at me and held out a pack of cigarettes. I raised my hand and shook my head. She extinguished her cigarette in an ashtray by the door. Then she kissed me on the cheek, took my hand, and strolled with me to her car.

'Why'd you leave me like that at the table?' I asked once we were sitting inside.

'I needed a little break,' she said, touching up her lipstick in the rearview mirror.

'I felt like an idiot just sitting there. I didn't know if you were coming back or what.'

'I lost track of time. I'm sorry.'

She put the keys in the ignition and was just about to turn them when I reached out and touched her hand. Her head snapped in my direction. I pulled the keys out of the ignition and locked eyes with her.

'You're going to have to stop playing games with me, lady.'

'I'm not playing games.' She reached for her keys, and I pulled back my hand.

'No?'

'Not at all. Now, please give those back to me.'

'What happened to him? To Teko?'

'I can't tell you.'

'Why not?'

'It's too terrible.'

'You remember our deal, don't you?' I handed the keys back to her. 'Total honesty.'

Beatrice shook her head and stuck the keys back in the ignition.

'Do you mind if we go somewhere else?' she said. 'I feel uncomfortable discussing this in a parking lot.

'Sure,' I said. 'Let's drive up the hill.'

A few minutes later we were looking at the city of Los Angeles from the viewing platform behind the Griffith Park Observatory, spread out below like a massive carpet of lights all the way to the horizon. Both of us were smoking now.

'I can't remember the last time I came up here,' she said. 'It's so beautiful.'

'It only looks beautiful from up here,' I said. 'Down there, not so much.'

Beatrice tossed a sidelong glance in my direction and looked back at the cityscape.

'They tracked us down,' she said after a moment, her eyes fixed on some point in the middle distance.

'Who did?'

'My father; my uncle, some other men. They got it in their heads Teko had kidnapped me. We were hiding in a village near the border of Zimbabwe. Teko knew some people there. But they found us. They showed up in the night and dragged Teko out of the shack where we were sleeping. It was horrible. My father made me watch as the others tied Teko's ankles and wrists. I screamed for them to stop. My father clamped a hand over my mouth, and one of my uncle's friends tied a rope around Teko's neck and strung him from a tree. I broke free from my father and begged for them to kill me too; it was as much my fault as Teko's. My uncle stuck a needle in my arm. The next thing I knew, I awoke in a hospital in Cape Town. And a few days later, I was back in Los Angeles. We never talked about it again.' She pressed out the cigarette on the wall, leaving a black smudge, and looked at me. 'You're the only person I've ever told.' There was a mix of pain and hate in her eyes as she held my gaze. 'I hope you're happy now.'

I could feel a tension building inside me as she'd told the story. It started in the pit of my stomach and worked its way into my chest and into my neck and shoulders. I'd been warned off this woman by my mother, by Concha, and I'd ignored them both. Now I saw how right they'd been.

I snatched her pack of cigarettes sitting on the wall and lit another with the end of the one I was finishing. 'And I remind you of him?'

'When I got back, I reinvented myself. I was determined not to let what happened in South Africa define me. I focused on my studies and the family's art holdings, and I've been damned successful at it. South Africa was a closed book, never to be opened again. Then you happened. The moment I laid eyes on that portrait of yours, *The Savior*, it all came back to me again, that image of the dying boy. And I found myself wishing I'd died with him too that night.'

'That's fucked up.'

'Yes. It is, isn't it?'

'How can you live under the same roof as your father?'

She crinkled her forehead at me.

'He killed your boyfriend.'

Beatrice shook her head vehemently. 'Someone else was responsible for Teko's murder. It took my father as much by surprise as it did me. He was only trying to protect me; he thought I was in danger.'

'He told you that?'

'Absolutely.'

'And you believe him?'

'Of course.'

'I hope he's being straight with you. I'd hate for him to get any strange ideas about me.'

14

Qurban

The day Anne's article came out, my classmates at LACC surprised me by congratulating me up and down the halls of the art building, waving copies of the magazine at me. I hadn't seen the article yet, nor had either Anne or Beatrice given me a heads-up as to when it would be coming out. So I borrowed a copy from a friend and paged over to the story. I was astonished to see my section was twice the length of what had been written about the other two artists. Anne had made me out to be some kind of Renaissance-man activist for LA's street people, recording life lived at the edge. She even compared me to Henri Toulouse-Lautrec toward the end of the article. Most astonishing of all, though, was a centerfold of me from the exhibition in my white guayabera standing next to *The Savior*.

That evening, my fellow artists mobbed me at the center's monthly roundtable meeting. I was touched by how happy they were for me, with some of them even asking me to autograph their copies of the magazine. At the end of the meeting, Lucinda presented me with a framed copy of the article and whispered in my ear that she wanted to see me in her office afterward. Then we all moved into the central exhibition space, which had been cleared for dancing and kitted out with chairs and tables laden with food people had brought for our potluck dinner.

I looked around for Sexto. Since he wasn't one of the artists, we never invited him to the roundtable meetings. But he always stuck around for the social afterwards. I realized as I looked for him I hadn't seen him for at least a week, if not two, which I found concerning, since he was so much a part of the center. None of the other artists had seen him, not even La Plumera, who Sexto was eternally pestering.

After dinner, I found Lucinda in her office, rifling through a stack of papers on her prized mid-century black shellac and brass credenza.

'Have you seen Sexto?' I asked from the open doorway.

She regarded me over her shoulder for a moment, then straightened up, a thick file folder in her hand. 'I was going to ask you the same thing.'

'Maybe we should call his house.'

'I tried, but the number we have on file's disconnected.'

I nodded. 'I'll go check on him. I'm sure he's all right.'

'Thank you. I meant to go myself. But I've had a million other things on my plate, including an offer from an anonymous patron I wanted to discuss with you.'

'What kind of offer?'

'A fully funded exhibition in Paris. We'd be joining forces with two other US inner-city art centers, plus a couple more in France. So six artists in total. You were specially requested.'

Of course, I was.

'When did this come up?' I asked

'This afternoon. I received a call from the patron's lawyer. It's still in the planning stages. There would be a sizeable donation to the center as part of the deal, which we could really use for facilities and for the children's art center I've been planning.'

'Well done, Lucinda. I'm happy for you.'

Lucinda peered at me for a beat.

'How do *you* feel about it? About going to Paris.'

'I'd have to talk to my mother. I don't like leaving her alone for too long.'

'I'm surprised you're not more excited. It's a fantastic opportunity.'

'What's the catch, Lucinda?'

She placed the file folder on her desk and crossed her arms. 'There's no catch. Just one condition.'

I spread my lips into a humorless smile. There always *was* a condition, wasn't there?

'The patron gets to select the paintings that get exhibited. In your case, they specifically requested your self-portrait, the one that appears in the article.'

'I don't have that one anymore.'

'I've already put in a call to the buyer, Ms. Schein. She's agreed to loan the paintings for the Paris exhibition.'

'Maybe she's the patron.'

Lucinda shook her head. 'Definitely not her.'

* * *

I jogged over the bridge to Sexto's and rounded his grandmother's house to his bungalow in the back, a cute, whitewashed in-law unit nestled among flowering hibiscus plants and birds of paradise. I rapped a few times on his door and peered through the windows. The curtains were drawn but were thin enough for me to see the bed was unmade and the sink crammed with dirty dishes.

Pushing open the kitchen window, I slid inside and looked around the sparsely furnished apartment. Everything seemed normal except for the dripping bathtub tap. I went to turn it off and saw the tub was filled with rusty water. Then I went back to Sexto's bedroom and carefully inspected it. There were a few cobwebs here and there, including one stretching from a bedpost to a chair next to the bed.

I ran across the yard to his grandmother's house and knocked on the back door. It swung open on its own, and I stepped inside. A bad smell, like raw sewage, laced the air. I called out Sexto's grandmother's name and ran upstairs to her bedroom.

Creeping inside so as not to frighten here, I found her sleeping fitfully under the covers. The smell was particularly pungent in there. I looked around the room, which seemed tidy enough at first glance, trying to identify the source of the smell. The door to her bathroom was half-open, so I poked my head inside. The toilet had overflown, and the floor was filthy with human waste that had been tracked back into the bedroom. I turned and looked in horror at Sexto's grandmother and caught sight of her waste-encrusted slippers at the foot of her bed.

As I moved toward her bed, she jerked awake and stared at me with wide, fearful eyes, which stopped me in my tracks.

'*Señora*, it's me, Virgilio.'

She scooted back, squeezing up against the wall.

I held up my hand. 'It's okay, Señora, don't worry. I'm a friend. A friend of Sexto's. He sent me to check on you.'

She whimpered at the mention of Sexto's name and glanced about the room, as if searching for him.

'Donde esta mi Sexto?' she asked, switching to Spanish.

'He's at the art center, Señora. He had to work late.'

'Que han hecho con el?' she asked, raising her voice.

This last question made me feel suddenly panicky inside. What have they done with him?

'Nothing, Señora. He's perfectly fine,' I offered, grasping at straws, swiping away the cold sweat that had broken out on my forehead. I took a breath and gently added, 'When was the last time you saw him?'

'No me recuerdo... No me recuerdo!'

An hour later, the house was swarming with police officers, a social worker, a couple of paramedics from Los Angeles General Hospital, and a few neighbors. One officer took my statement, which included a missing person report regarding Sexto. Another officer lifted his head and looked at me sharply when I mentioned the tunnels as one possibility of where he might be. He stepped onto the porch and fired up his handheld radio while the officer interviewing me kept asking questions and writing notes. I could hear the squawk of the radio outside and the word 'tunnel' and feared I might have fucked up.

Meanwhile, the medics had moved Sexto's grandmother to the relative safety of her living room away from the toxic stink of the bathroom to finish their examination. The social worker hovered in the distance waiting to assess the situation. As Sexto was his grandmother's only next of kin, there was talk of what to do with her in his absence; she kept insisting she was okay to remain on her own and that Sexto would be home soon. One of her neighbors, a woman in her sixties from halfway down the block, volunteered to stay with her for a bit to make sure she got something to eat, while a couple of the other neighbors focused on cleaning up the apartment, starting with the bathroom.

Once I was sure the situation was under control, I excused myself and ran out the door, having promised Sexto's grandmother I'd return the next day to check on her. It was already ten o'clock.

I ran as fast as I could to the tunnels. It had been almost a month and a half since I was last there. The new guy standing guard at the entrance said he didn't know anything when I asked him about Sexto. The code word had changed since I'd last been there. But he stepped aside and allowed me access in exchange for a pack of cigarettes.

I dropped into the tunnel and hurried in the direction of Molly's, where Sexto liked to hang out. As I followed the tunnel around, I ran straight into Bruce Lee and Sexto. They were feeding the flaming oil barrels nearest the main cross path between two of the largest side tunnels. Both of them were dressed in black jumpsuits with red bandanas tied around their heads. My relief at seeing Sexto was quickly replaced by fear at the sight of a nasty bruise on his right cheek and scabbed-over scratches on his forehead. He dropped his stack of newspapers when I went to hug him and looked through me with a dull expression in his eyes. His breath smelled of cheap alcohol. I peered into his eyes and repeated his name and held him close for a second.

Bruce Lee stamped his foot, and I looked up. He pointed in the direction of Molly's toward the back of that section of the tunnel. Three men were walking in our direction, two white guys not much older than me in blue jeans and Polo shirts, and a tall Latino guy probably in his early thirties wearing a dark suit with no tie whom I'd never seen before. I stepped away from Sexto as they reached us.

'These boys are working,' the tall guy said. 'Why don't you come with me?'

'I need to take this one home.' I nodded at Sexto. 'His grandmother's sick.'

One of the Polo shirt guys flicked open a switchblade and held it at his side. I glared at him, memorizing every detail of his face. Short blonde hair, buzzed high over his ears; clean shaven; long chin, high cheekbones, flat nose, almond-shaped brown eyes; pale, pimply complexion.

'We can talk about it my office,' the tall guy said. He waved a hand at the guy with the switchblade, who shut the blade.

'Seriously, man.' I put my hand on Sexto's arm and caught the slightest flicker of a reaction in his eyes. 'He's his grandmother's caregiver. She's not doing well. He needs to come home.'

'I won't repeat my invitation,' the tall guy said. 'I recommend you accept it before someone has an accident.'

He held out his hand to me. There was a smile on his face. It sent a shiver of fear the length of my spine. His teeth were showing. Cleft chin, thick lower lip, well-groomed mustache, Indian nose, black eyes,

Groucho Marx eyebrows, one-inch scar on his left cheek, crow-black hair, medium length, parted in the middle. I followed him, flanked on either side by the Polo-shirted guys. I glanced back at Sexto and Bruce Lee, who had returned to their task.

Just past Molly's, we ducked into a smaller side tunnel and carried on down a narrow corridor, then turned left through an open doorway and into a square room that was fitted out like a plush executive office complete with wall-to-wall dark blue shag carpet. Aside from the antique wooden desk at the back of the room facing the door, there was also a black leather sofa and a wet bar.

'Sit there.' The tall man moved around to the other side of the big desk and pointed at a chair in front of it. He remained standing even after I sat down. 'Hand your backpack to Yuri.'

Mr. Switchblade stepped up to me, and I handed him my backpack. He opened it and dug around inside. After a moment, he pulled out my sketchpad and tossed it to the man behind the desk who sat down and leafed through it.

'My friend needs to come home.'

'Don't worry. He'll go home eventually.' He turned the sketchpad ninety degrees and studied one of the sketches, then he flipped the page. 'He's working off a debt he owes us. In the meantime, he's got room and board down here, and even a bit of entertainment if he's a good boy.'

He turned the sketchbook around and showed me one of my drawings of Carino.

'I wanted to have a word with you about this one.'

'What kind of a debt?' I asked, keeping on subject.

He held out the sketch to me and tapped his finger against it. 'I understand from this young man that you've been interfering.'

'How much does Sexto owe you?'

He put the pad face down on his desk. 'Your friend was entrusted with something he was meant to take good care of. He failed us. So we've put him to work.'

'How much?'

'It's not about the money. At least not in this case. It's about the principle.'

'I'll work off his debt. He's got to go home.'

He picked up the pad and held it out to me again. 'I'll discuss your offer with management. In the meantime, I want to talk to you about this one. Did you tell him he should quit the cockfight?'

'He's only seventeen.'

'Is he a member of your family?'

'No.'

'A friend?'

'What's your point?'

'I understand you took him after hours to the Paradiso Bar and plied him with beer and marijuana, this minor you're so concerned about.'

The guy was still smiling at me. It felt like an icebox in the room. My face was hot, and sweat was trickling into my eyes. I wiped my forehead dry with my shirtsleeve.

'You're what, twenty? Twenty-one?' he asked.

'Twenty.'

'Right. An adult. What else did you do with this minor?'

'I didn't do anything? We just talked.'

'You just talked...'

'I felt sorry for him. He's from Cuba, like my mother. His family drowned trying to get here. He's a smart kid. I was just telling him he could do better if he went to school.'

He nodded at Yuri, who disappeared from the room. The other Polo-shirted guy fell into place at my side.

'My name's Leo, by the way. I'm the new superintendent. I'll be down here a lot more than the last one.'

'How does the King fit into all this?'

Leo clasped his hands on the desk and leaned forward. 'Why don't you let me ask the questions?'

Yuri walked back into the room followed by Carino, who was wearing a white Polo shirt, black Levis, and a pair of white deck shoes. His hair was cut short and had a healthy sheen to it. There was a thin gold chain around his neck and a gold bracelet on his wrist. Leo pushed back from his desk and held out a hand to him, and Carino walked over and stood next to his chair. Leo reached up and stroked his arm, and Carino stared at me with a fierce look in his eye.

'Is this the one you were telling me about?' Leo asked him in Spanish. Carino nodded.

'Tell me again what you told me about the night he took you to the Paradiso.'

'He gave me drugs. He kissed me on the mouth and invited me to his apartment.'

Leo lowered his hand to Carino's crotch and fondled him. I looked up at Carino, who glanced down at Leo's hand. His jaw was tense.

'Did he touch you like this?' Leo asked.

Carino looked back at me and nodded. An erection was filling out his jeans.

I leapt up from my chair and the Polo-shirted guy hauled me back into it by the scuff of my neck. 'Why are you doing this?' I said to Carino, shaking off my handler. 'I never touched you! I was trying to help you.'

'You're a faggot and a liar,' Carino growled, his face turning red. 'I hope they cut off your balls and stuff them down your throat.'

'Okay, that's enough,' Leo said. He tapped Carino's ass, and Carino followed Yuri out of the room.

'It's not true,' I said. 'I didn't touch him.'

Leo shrugged. 'Doesn't matter. He'll say whatever I tell him. The point is you should leave well enough alone. Mind your own business.

And' — He held up the sketchpad — 'no more drawings like this.'

He flipped through the pad and ripped out my drawings of the cockfight and handed them to the Polo-shirted guy, who turned them into streamers.

'And no more paintings of the things you see down here either.'

He reached into one of the drawers of his desk and pulled out a feather, exactly like the one I'd found on my nightstand, and twirled it in his fingers.

'I'll trust you to destroy the painting you've been working on at the art center for the past month, that beautiful one of the cockfight.'

'How about if I donate it to you? It'll look nice on these bare walls.'

Leo arched an eyebrow at me.

'I hate to destroy art. Especially my own.'

Yuri walked back into the room and stood next to me. Leo rose from his chair.

'I'll discuss your offers with management. Both of them. Come back tomorrow night. Bring the painting.'

'I haven't finished it yet.'

Leo nodded at Yuri, who responded by pulling me to my feet by my arm. In that instant, I caught sight of a pair of sculptures, about knee-high, displayed next to the credenza behind Leo's desk. They were well near identical to Lucinda's found-art towers in the reception room at the art center. Leo looked at them and back at me. I couldn't believe I hadn't noticed the family resemblance before. I flashed my teeth at Leo.

'Talk about *All in the Family*, homeboy...' I said.

'Steady,' Leo responded. 'You'd do best to keep anything you see down here to yourself from now on.' He pointed at the door. 'We're done. See you tomorrow.'

Yuri stepped aside to make room for me. I nodded and moved to the door.

'One last thing, Mr. Savior,' Leo said.

I turned around.

'Don't talk to the cops again.'

Yuri and his Polo-shirted twinsy marched me out of the tunnels and watched as I climbed up the access stairs. My brain gyrated with everything that had just happened the whole way back to Sexto's grandmother's house. The more I thought about it, the more I felt I had to do something. Somehow I had to save Sexto and keep myself safe at the same time. But the tentacles of it all were boggling my mind. Where did one thing start and the other end? No place was safe anymore, not my apartment, not the art center, and everyone seemed to have a hand in what was happening, including Beatrice, her father, Anne, Lucinda, Concha, even the police. The only person I could trust was my mother. And I was even starting to get paranoid about her.

When I arrived at Sexto's grandmother's house, I found her neighbor curled up on the sofa in the living room, watching a late-night Spanish soap on TV. She'd agreed with the social worker to take care of her for a couple of days while the county investigated what should be done if Sexto didn't return. The house had been cleaned up, and Sexto's grandmother was asleep in her bedroom. I reassured the neighbor that Sexto would be back in a couple of days and offered to stay the rest of the night. But she declined. She lived only a couple of houses away, she told me, and it was no problem for her to pop back and forth during the day. Nighttime was critical, though, and she had promised the social worker she would stay with Sexto's grandmother throughout the night, just in case. So I went home and fell into bed with my clothes on, angry and exhausted, passing out as soon as my head touched the sheets.

15

Dilogún

At some point in the early hours of the morning, the sound of my mother's chanting awakened me from a deep, dreamless slumber. It was low and rhythmic and soothing and coming from just on the other side of my bedroom door. I reckoned she was communing with her orisha, Changó. Keeping my eyes closed, I let the vibrations of her chant wash over me and bathe me in their radiance — warm, moist, prickly; ochre, crimson, black; then white-hot as the sun that blazes above us — refocusing it all into my forehead, just as she had taught me, right behind the bridge of my nose, to collide with the storehouse of my spiritual energy, my aché. In that instant of connection, the sound of blackbirds approaching echoed in my brain — the vigoration of a thousand pairs of wings — and my spirit began to lift out of my body, preparing to travel. Just at the point of separation — that unmistakable tight stretch of the spiritual umbilical right before the final severing — my mother's chanting changed pitch, the vibrations slowed, and my spirit splashed back into my physical coil, shocking me awake.

Flipping onto my side, I peered into the darkness, at the crack between the dark brown planks of my wooden floor and my bedroom door above it, and was surprised to see the flicker-flutter of shuffling feet moving across the dim candlelight illuminating our living room. Then came the familiar clicking sounds of cowrie shells being cast onto a ceremonial mat. *What the fuck?* I shot a glance at my wall clock and felt the bottom drop out of my stomach. My mother was conducting a spiritual reading, a *dilogún* — at three o'clock in the morning? In the middle of our living room?

I threw off my covers and pulled on a pair of thin, white sweats that doubled as pyjamas, and went for the door. But just as I reached out to grab the handle, I saw it was glowing yellow-red, and I pulled back my hand just in time to avoid searing it on the hot brass. I took a few deep, calming breaths, and, surrendering to my mother's will, sank to the floor and sat with my back against the door. A thin trail of cigar smoke wafted into my room from under the door, and I heard my mother softly chanting the initiatory prayer to *Eleguá*, the undisputed master of the orishas. Then the room went quiet, and I heard a voice I never expected to hear in my apartment ever again.

'What happens now?' I heard Beatrice Schein ask. I held my breath for the thirty seconds it took for my mother to answer.

'*Hija*,' my mother said with uncharacteristic tenderness, 'Santería is unlike any religion you may be familiar with.'

Why was she calling Beatrice hija? I wondered.

'I'm not familiar with *any* religion,' Beatrice responded.

'No?'

'Not really. Only what I've heard from others. My father's an atheist.'

'And your mother?'

Beatrice let out a humourless chuckle. 'She doesn't really have a say.'

My mother spit out a mild oath in Lucumí, voicing her disapproval. 'You're in for an education, hija. By the time I'm finished with you, you'll have much more than a say.'

'That's why I'm here,' Beatrice said, or something like that. The volume of her voice had dropped so low that I could barely make out anything she was saying.

'Good! Here's your first lesson, hija, before we begin the dilogún: In other religions, God is distant and impersonal — up in the sky somewhere.' I pictured my mother waving her cigar at the ceiling.

'Sounds a lot like my father.'

'Hush! Students listen first and talk later.'

'I'm sorry.'

'In Santería, we have a close, personal relationship with our gods, the orishas.'

'You have more than one?'

'I said hush! One more outburst like that and we're finished for the night.'

I was half-expecting for Beatrice to grab her purse and go. But she remained silent and, after a moment of pause, my mother continued.

'We santeros do not cower before our gods. We speak with them, listen to them, and, more importantly, we follow their guidance. And the main way we receive guidance from the orishas is through divination, through dilogún. The orishas speak to us through these cowrie shells.' I heard the clicking again, as my mother ran her fingers over the shells. 'Each of these shells has been opened, consecrated and empowered to speak for the orishas. Tonight, you'll be consulting Eleguá, the master. Later, once we determine the identity of your own personal orisha, you'll consult with him or with her. Understood?'

I didn't hear any response from Beatrice, so I assumed she answered yes with a nod of her head.

'Excellent,' my mother said. 'Now, when I cast the shells, ask Eleguá your question or tell him your problem. He will speak to you through me and reveal the energy pattern that is currently taking place in your life. He will point out what crossroad you are at on your path to destiny, and will let you know whether you are in a state of balance or imbalance.

If you are in a state of imbalance, Eleguá will identify the source of that imbalance and will recommend rituals and sacrifices you can offer to alter your destiny and put you back on track to a state of balance. Do you have any questions, hija? Before I cast the shells?'

'Yes,' Beatrice said softly, almost as if through tears, 'the rituals and sacrifices you mentioned, to get me back on track... you're not talking about magic, are you?'

'There is magic, yes, to be sure. But you don't need magic to regain balance, hija. The power is already within you. It's in all of us. But sometimes we need a little help from the gods to find it and to take back control. Eleguá will help you find it.'

A quiet sobbing emanated from the other side of the door, and I felt embarrassed to listen any further to what was clearly something very personal taking place between Beatrice and my mother. Snatching up a cigarette, I stepped out of my room onto the fire escape landing and lit up, flicking the burning match over the rail and watching it drop onto the cracked sidewalk below before taking a drag. I was feeling dysregulated by what was developing in my living room. This was not just some ordinary spiritual consultation, the kind I'd seen my mother conduct over the years with the members of our community. She had called Beatrice hija, daughter, for God's sake! That same woman she had described as dark and had warned me against a few days before. I didn't get it. But, with so much on my plate already, I decided some things were best left to one side. So I drew a mental curtain over the whole thing, drew another deep drag on my cigarette, and forced myself to focus on what I had to do later that day. I had Sexto to save.

16

Changó

That morning, I skipped class and went straight to the art center following an uncomfortable breakfast with my mother, which went something like this:

'Finish your food.'

'What was she doing here, Mamá?'

My mother lifted her shoulders. 'She asked to see me, and I saw her.'

'At three in the morning? What did she want?'

'Consultations are confidential, hijo. You know that.' She pointed at my half-eaten fried egg, the dark yellow yolk dribbling onto the plate and staining the toast. 'Don't let that go to waste.'

'Never mind the food.' I moved the plate to one side. 'You said to keep away from her! She's dark inside, you said.'

'I know more about the situation than I did before. Now mind your own business and go do what you must.'

She held my gaze for a long moment, punctuating her last comment with the weight of silence, then started to gather up the dishes. But I held my place and, focusing my eyes on her hands, willed her to put down the dishes and face me.

'What is it, mijo?' Her voice was weary, her eyes bloodshot and tired.

'There's more to this story, isn't there?'

She let out a long breath and sat back down. 'She's interested in coming again to la reunion.' She raised her eyebrows and pulled her mouth to one side.

'You mean as a participant?'

My mother nodded. 'She felt the spirit of Oshún the last time. She wants to experience it again. On Wednesday night. I believe she's an old soul.'

'I thought you didn't like her.'

'It's not a bad thing to keep her close. I can control things better that way' — she stood up — 'now that that ugly world is sucking you in.'

'I see. So was it *your* idea or hers?'

I never received an answer to my question. The conversation was over. My mother chanted a rhythmic prayer and gently danced to the kitchen balancing the dishes in her hand.

Fifteen minutes later, I was knocking on the door to Lucinda's office. I waited a couple of seconds before trying the doorknob. It was unlocked. I poked my head inside and found it empty. Her telephone was flashing with an incoming call. I struggled against the urge to search her desk for evidence of her involvement with Leo. But I thought the better of it, not wanting to be accused of burglary, or worse. So I withdrew just in time to see her walking toward me holding a steaming cup of coffee. She didn't act surprised to see me there so early in the day.

'I found Sexto,' I said, once we were in her office. I searched her face for some clue as to whether Leo had said anything to her about the night before. But it was difficult to read her. 'He should be back in a couple of days.'

'Wonderful,' she responded absently, paging through some papers on her desk. Her telephone was no longer blinking. 'It's lucky for me we have a couple of other more responsible assistants.'

'Don't you want to know where he was?'

Lucinda shook her head. 'I'm not sure I'll be keeping him around.'

'His grandmother's being taken care of.'

Lucinda looked up at me, her lips hardening into a stony smile. 'How can I help you, Virgilio?'

'I've been thinking about the Paris exhibition.'

'And?'

'I'll be happy to participate. You can tell your patron that she or he can count on my cooperation.'

'I'm happy to hear it, Virgilio.'

She extended her hand toward me, and I shook it. It felt cold.

'Is it Leo?' I asked.

Lucinda pulled back her hand and cut her eyes at me.

'Doesn't matter,' I said. 'I was just curious. Still, if I were you, I'd be careful where you get the funding for your children's center. You wouldn't want the other donors to get wind of anything shady.'

'Be careful, Virgilio.' Lucinda swiveled her chair around and faced her desk. 'Don't go pulling at threads. The whole garment could fall apart.'

'It's always about the money, isn't it?'

'Money makes the world go around. Isn't that what they say?'

I shook my head at the cliché and at her head bobbing over her papers.

'Yeah, maybe. But it doesn't have to be dirty money or blood money.'

Lucinda turned back around. Her face was red, and the tips of her nostrils were flaring.

'I've been the director of this center for over five years and a mother. I don't need lectures from someone who just graduated from high school a year ago. And for your information, I would never knowingly do anything to endanger this center or my liberty.'

I leaned forward and spoke in a lowered voice. 'Lucinda, I'm not lecturing you. I'm speaking to you confidentially about a concern I have for me, for you, for the center. I'm not planning on shooting off my mouth. But I won't be silenced either, by you or anyone. If you have a problem with that, let me know, and I'll take my stuff and go.'

Lucinda leaned back and looked at me over the top of her glasses, then shook her head and waved her hand dismissively. 'We'll talk later, mijo. I've got a lot to do this morning.'

I left her office clueless as to how much she knew about Leo or what he was up to. Maybe she'd only spoken to him about me or had shown him my work. But that didn't explain her reluctance to talk about him or her cryptic comment about pulling at threads.

When I got to my storage cupboard, I was surprised to find the lock hanging open. I reflected on the night before, trying to remember whether I'd secured it. I'd left the center so quickly; it was possible I'd forgotten to do so. But it wasn't like me to be absent-minded, even when under stress.

I inspected the lock. The numbers were scrambled just as I always left them. As far as I was aware, no one else knew the combination. Not wanting to get paranoid, I pushed it all out of my mind and took out my supplies and the unfinished cockfight painting.

I set up in a quiet corner and stared at the board. I'd arranged the spectators in an amphitheatrical semicircle fronting the area from where the competitors emerged. The figures in the foreground were showing the backs of their heads. And those standing at the sides expressed the emotions of the fight: excitement, frustration, shock, bloodlust. Wide eyes, contorted mouths, clenched fists. A tattered feather floating in the middle, glowing as if from an internal light, and a few discreetly placed droplets of blood splashing upward, were the only clues as to what kind of event they were witnessing. And over it all, I'd painted a dark, vaulted ceiling. That bit was still unfinished.

I pulled out my brushes and paints and spent the next few hours working on the painting. In the ceiling, high above the scene, I painted the protective image of Changó, king and warrior, his ax raised heavenward, his legs spread wide. I blended him into the vaulting, like a kind of medieval gargoyle.

When I finished with the ceiling, I took a break and went to the vending machine to buy a chocolate bar and a cup of coffee. Then I came back and sat in a folding chair across from the painting, alternating between munching on the chocolate bar and staring at the tableau, trying to see it as if for the first time. I was pleased to see that even with the addition of Changó, the feather remained the focus of the painting. It was only if you looked for Changó that you could see him staring down at the men, defiant, ready to strike.

Then I started on the most critical addition to the painting. In the shadowy background, I worked on incorporating the image of a woman dressed in flowing robes, a turban on her head, her eyes wide, her mouth puckered and blowing a mist toward the feather. I struggled a bit with the image; I wanted it to be barely visible, just the ghost of an image; there for those who know where to look. I didn't want anything to detract from the subject of the painting — the feather. I tested the image of the woman several times on an extra piece of board until I was satisfied I'd perfected the technique. Then I attacked the painting itself.

Other artists drifted in and out of the center over the course of the next few hours. A couple of them strolled by and checked out what I was working on. We knew better than to interrupt each other when we were in the zone working on something. But it was normal to have someone look over your shoulder as long as they didn't linger for too long. Feeling a pang of hunger, I checked my watch and was surprised to see it was already three in the afternoon. I still had a bit more to do. Something wasn't quite right about one of the woman's hands. But I had to eat something. So I covered up the painting and went down the road to a taco truck parked a couple of blocks away.

* * *

Schein's driver was waiting for me when I arrived at the tunnel entrance that night. Unlike our ride from the Westside a few weeks earlier, our journey to Schein's Century City offices was made in complete silence, except for a couple of French-accented grunts in answer to my questions about where we were going.

We accessed Schein's tower via the underground parking lot and rode the elevator to the 44th floor, which his investment company occupied in its entirety. Then I followed the driver past the deserted reception area and empty corridors to a large office where Schein was waiting for me, dressed in a light blue linen suit with no tie and black alligator skin shoes.

Two of the four walls were all glass, which provided a dizzying southwest-facing view of West Los Angeles. The city was ablaze with light. Schein offered me a seat and a drink, which his driver poured for me before leaving the two of us alone, facing each other across Schein's massive glass-topped executive desk.

'On a clear afternoon, one can see all the way to the Pacific.' He indicated the view with a sweep of his hand.

I nodded and glanced around the office at Schein's collection of paintings, sculpture, and traditional eastern art, including works by Dali and Chagall, a medieval triptych painted on wood, a beautifully framed batik, and a Xi'an Terracotta Warrior.

'I was hoping you'd bring yours.' He pointed at an unoccupied space on the wall to the left of his desk. 'I had that area cleared for it earlier today.'

'I was waiting for Leo to tell me whether my offer had been accepted. Plus, I intended for it to hang on the wall of his office — in the tunnels.'

'We've accepted both of your offers.' He glanced at his wristwatch, a Santos de Cartier. 'Your associate should be on his way home by now if he's not there already.'

'Thank you. His grandmother was sick, and he's her only living relative and caregiver. If I hadn't checked in on her when I did, she might have died.'

'I wasn't aware. I'm sorry for that.'

'I told Leo.'

'Well, it's resolved nonetheless. In any event, we were impressed by your bravery. I'll make arrangements with the art center to pick up the painting, which, I believe, was the other component of your offer. I'll display it here, especially as our tunnel project will be liquidated shortly and the various entertainments relocated.'

'When do I start working off Sexto's debt?'

Schein shook his head. 'We're prepared to forgive the debt in its entirety in exchange for a few simple promises from you.'

'I'm not selling my soul to you if that's what you expect, Mr. Schein. I'd rather work off the debt.'

'It's nothing like that at all, young man. Besides, the existence of the soul is a myth. The sooner you learn that, the more quickly you'll rise in this world.'

'With the greatest of respect, Mr. Schein, I'll pass on the philosophy lesson.'

Schein shrugged. 'One should never refuse instruction from those who are more experienced and successful. But then again, you're still very young. In time you'll realize that what I'm saying is true.'

'Maybe.' I took a sip of my drink and set aside the glass. 'What are your conditions?'

'I admire your pragmatism.'

'It has its limits. Your conditions...?'

'Fine. I've agreed with my daughter to help fund a European exhibition of inner-city art she's curating, which will preview in New York in the spring and move on to Paris thereafter. The exhibition will feature three artists, including two painters — you're one of them — and a sculptor. By design, your paintings will feature prominently in the hopes they'll catch the attention of the right people in the art world.'

He paused and waited for my reaction. Even though I tried to keep it out of my face, I was excited by the additional details he was providing and felt suddenly breathless. I took another sip of my drink and nodded.

'I heard about the tour from the director of the center. I'm definitely interested.'

'You won't have another opportunity like it, I assure you. Your participation in the project will lift your profile overnight to the international level. What you do with that will be up to you. Ultimately, the opportunity will be yours to exploit or to squander. Which brings me to the conditions.'

I leaned forward.

'First, you will no longer paint or exhibit anything you've witnessed in the tunnels, particularly in the rather sensitive section of the complex that you stumbled into the other night with your associate.'

'My mind's a complete blank about that night, I can assure you.'

'Be that as it may, my condition stands; second, you will henceforth absent yourself from the tunnels unless we've requested your presence there; third, you will keep what you've seen in the tunnels entirely confidential; and fourth, and most critically, you will refrain from involving yourself romantically with my daughter.'

I remained quiet for a moment, trying to process Schein's conditions.

'Needless to say,' Schein continued, 'my daughter knows nothing of my projects downtown. I'm hoping to keep it that way.'

'What makes you think I'd get involved with your daughter? She's nearly ten years older than me and way out of my league.'

Schein narrowed his eyes at me. 'I would agree with that assessment, young man. But my daughter has a romantic streak. It colors many of her decisions; her decision to champion your work as well, I imagine. So I'm counting on you to discourage any slippage of your working relationship into the personal.'

'She's not my type anyway.'

'I know how these things work, young man. She's an attractive woman; you're a young man in his prime, and art touches on the emotions. But make no mistake; I will not forgive any of that if you violate this particular condition.'

I stood and stretched my legs. Schein looked up at me from his desk then rose to his full height.

'I'll do my best,' I said.

'I'll need a promise.'

'I told you I wasn't going to sell my soul, Mr. Schein. That's the best you're going to get from me.'

Schein regarded me for a moment with a deadpan expression, then slowly made his way around from behind his desk and stood in front of it, folding his arms across his chest.

'We have big plans for your neighborhood,' he said. 'That rat-infested place you call home.'

'Who's we?'

Schein waved his hand. 'Doesn't matter. The point is, there's a lot of money to be made once the subway is installed. We'll be tearing down most everything east of Alameda to the LA River, and north-to-south from 1st Street to 7th Street — to make way for high-end condominiums, world-class museums. We're going to call it the Downtown Los Angeles Arts District.'

I lifted my chin in an impotent show of bravado. 'What's that got to do with me?'

'You live there, don't you?'

I nodded.

'If you cooperate, there will be big opportunities for you, a high-profile, local artist; if you oppose me, you'll be out on the street. I'll make sure the first building torn down is yours, and next will be that bridge I'm told you're so fond of.'

My heart skipped a beat at the mention of the bridge, and I drew a deep breath in an effort to maintain control of my emotions.

'That's the look I was waiting for,' Schein said, with a gleam in his eyes. He glanced at his wristwatch and looked back up at me. 'Now then...your promise.'

My face flushed hot. The man had me. 'Yes,' I rasped, swiping at a trickle of sweat coursing down the side of my face. 'You have my promise.'

17

Sexto

Sexto was in his grandmother's kitchen when I arrived. He had just put her to bed and was in the middle of cleaning up. His hair had grown out and was a mess; there were dark circles under his eyes, and his cheeks were sunken. One of Leo's thugs had approached him earlier that evening when he was in the middle of stoking the oil barrels and had said, 'go home,' without any explanation. The last thing he'd said to Sexto as he scrambled up the ladder was 'don't you *ever* come back here.'

I brought Sexto up to speed about everything that had happened until then, including the status of his grandmother with the social worker, leaving out the part about Schein's threats. Sexto looked at the floor and nodded every so often as I spoke, then he sat at the kitchen table and took a deep breath, tears filling his eyes and spilling down his cheeks. I boiled water and made him some chamomile tea.

'Can you stay over?' He breathed in the earthy-sweet aroma of the tea. 'Just for tonight.'

'Yeah, of course. But I'll need to leave early. I've got class tomorrow morning, and I want to stop by home first to check on my mother.' I massaged his neck while he drank his tea and followed him out back to his bungalow.

Sexto had a double bed, just large enough to fit the two of us without much more room for turning over. I sat cross-legged on it, sketching in my pad while I waited for him to come out of the shower. It was a sketch of him standing on the 6th Street Bridge, screaming out his lungs over the viaduct.

He popped out of his bathroom a few minutes later, a towel around his waist, running a comb through his wet hair. He was skinnier than I remembered, almost like a concentration camp victim, with his ribcage showing. He sat on the bed next to me and leaned back against one of the pillows.

'Remember this?' I handed him the sketchpad and got up from the bed.

Sexto chuckled over the sketch of himself as I went into the bathroom to shower. A few minutes later when I came out in my towel, I found him under the covers waiting for me. My sketchbook was closed and on his nightstand.

'I'd offer you one of my *calzones*, but I don't wear any.' He sniggered.

'You don't expect me to sleep in the nude with you, do you?'

Sexto shrugged. 'Only if you want. It's not like I haven't seen you naked before.' He pointed at the bottom drawer of his clothes chest. 'There's a pair of P.E. shorts in there. It's up to you.'

I pulled the P.E. shorts out of the drawer, red satin with a gold stripe down the side, and peered at them. They were going to be a tight fit. But I didn't want to give Sexto any ideas. So I dropped my towel and struggled into them.

'Oh, my fucking ...' Sexto covered his mouth and laughed into his hands. 'They look painted on. I can totally see your family jewels.'

I slipped under the covers next to him.

'You're lucky to be so blessed in that department,' Sexto said, still laughing. 'Must be your black half.'

'Okay, enough,' I said, pulling up the covers tight to discourage Sexto from peeking under them.

I reached over to switch off the light on the nightstand, and Sexto touched my shoulder.

'Not yet,' he said. The laughter had gone out of his face. 'I want to talk a little bit.' There was a sad, hollow look in his eye.

'Sure, anything you want.'

'Is it okay if I rest my head against your chest while I talk?'

I smiled at him. 'Consider me your pillow.'

Sexto wriggled up against me and put his head on my chest, and I pulled him close. His hair was still damp and emanated the herby scent of his shampoo. He rested his hand on my stomach and ran his fingers through my belly hair as he spoke.

'They kept me down there for ten days. It was horrible.'

'Why? What did you do to them?'

Sexto buried his face in my chest for a long drawn-out moment until I thought he had passed out. Then he lifted his head and locked eyes with me. 'You know they're running drugs down there, don't you?' he whispered.

'It doesn't surprise me.'

'Well, they are. Under the main tunnel, there's a smaller one that extends all of the way to San Pedro, the one we fell into that other night. They bring in the stuff through there. The shit that happens in the main tunnel above is just a distraction, Molly's, the gambling, the fight clubs, all of that.'

'And that has something to do with you, because...?'

'When they caught us in the tunnel, they offered me money to keep quiet if I ran a couple of deliveries for them.'

'Shit.'

'I don't know what happened. I delivered the stuff to the wrong guy or ... '

'Or what?'

'Or, maybe I used some of it myself and shorted the guy on the delivery.'

'Sexto!'

'I know, I know, I'm a total idiot, a fucking pendejo.' Sexto slapped the side of his head and started sobbing.

'Hey, hang on.' I took hold of his hand and pulled him close. 'Just take it easy, mijo. Relax.'

Sexto's sobs subsided into a whimper.

'You're out now, so there's nothing to worry about.' I said. 'I've taken care of everything.'

'Thank you, Virgilio.' He wiped his face and looked up at me. 'What did you have to do?'

'Never mind that. Did they hurt you?'

'Only one time in the beginning when I tried to escape. That little bastard Bruce Lee ran to tell them I was going up one of the back ladders. I don't even want to say what they did to me. They threw me into the hole for I don't know how long before letting me out and telling me next time it would be worse. Then one of those Polo guys took me to Molly's and made me do sex stuff with one of the old ones while he watched. He said it was his way of making it up to me for sticking me in the hole.' Sexto closed his eyes and shook his head. 'It was disgusting. I couldn't even get it up. But he wouldn't let me leave there until I finished. So I did my best to think about someone else just to get through it. It's weird to say it. I used to like going to Molly's before. But they used it as a kind of torture. Twice a day I got blown at Molly's by the ugliest or freakiest ones.'

Sexto looked up at me as I hadn't reacted or said anything in response to what he'd been telling me. The truth is I was stunned by what had happened to him.

'Were there others?' I asked. 'Down there like you?'

Sexto nodded. 'Yeah, there were about eight of us, all guys, including Bruce Lee. We slept in a sort of stable they set up, each of us in a little cubicle. Someone was always standing guard to make sure we didn't talk to each other. So I don't know much about the rest except the guards had their favorites and treated some of us better than the others. But we were all slaves anyway.'

'Was one of them Carino?'

Sexto's head jerked up. 'You mean Leo's boy toy? Fucking pendejo! I should have bashed his head in when I had a chance.'

'Hey, hey...'

'Sorry...' Sexto let out a breath and shook his head. 'But I swear, Virgilio, that guy wanted to kill me. I could see it in his face, you know, like real murder, every time he laid eyes on me.' Tears stood out in his eyes. 'Why does he hate me so much? What did I ever do to him?'

'Don't worry about it now. You're safe as long as you don't get involved with those people anymore. And don't tell anyone about what happened to you, okay?'

Sexto nodded. 'Thanks for getting me out of there, Virgilio.'

'I've got your back, mijo.'

Sexto brought his hand up to my chest and gently massaged my pectorals.

'You were the one I thought about when they were forcing me to do stuff at Molly's.'

'It's okay. All kinds of weird shit happens in people's heads when they're being tortured. Don't worry about it.'

'I'm not worried.' He kissed me on the cheek and moved his hand down my chest, past my abs, and toward the waistband of the shorts.

I grabbed both his shoulders and moved him on to his back and moved my face close to his. 'You're tired, mijo. Plus, you've just gone through a traumatic time. Why don't you just rest and let your body and mind recover before you make things even more complicated.'

'You don't want to?'

'Trust me on this, mijo. Give the sex stuff a rest. I'll help you find someone you can safely talk to about all this shit. A professional. And keep taking good care of your abuelita.' I kissed him on the forehead. 'Now, face the wall and rest.'

* * *

I found Beatrice at the art center that afternoon sitting with Lucinda in her office. Lucinda was wearing her standard coveralls; Beatrice looked good enough to eat. White blouse, dark blue skirt, spiky heels, hair pulled away from her face. I lifted my hand at them in a quick greeting, and Lucinda invited me inside. Beatrice announced she'd selected a date in the spring for our tour and was there to work out some of the logistics. She wanted to chat with me after her meeting with Lucinda to discuss the pieces I'd be exhibiting. Nothing in her manner gave any hint she'd been consorting with my mother.

I set up in my usual corner and started on a new painting based on the drawing I'd sketched of Sexto the night before, screaming into the night on the bridge. I'd decided to work in acrylic this time and was on my knees priming the canvas when I saw Beatrice coming out of Lucinda's office. I stood and wiped my hands on a rag as she crossed the room in my direction.

'How've you been, Virgilio?'

'I heard you visited my mother the other night.'

'I dreamt of her again,' she said quietly. 'I wanted to talk to her about it.'

I noticed a thin, multicolored beaded amulet around her wrist.

'Did she give you that?' I pointed at the amulet.

Beatrice touched a finger to it and nodded. 'I'll be joining for another ceremony.'

'So I heard. Whose idea was that?'

'You have no idea how I felt the night we went. This rush of warmth, a loving energy that started here—' She touched the center of her forehead with her index finger, '—and spread throughout my body to the tips of my fingers and toes. I felt connected to the universe. I need to feel that again.'

'Why didn't you mention this before, the last time we saw each other?'

'It all seemed a bit mad. It took a while to process it. I felt confused. But everything became clear when I consulted with your mother.'

'I'm glad for you. But, so that you know, I won't be joining next time. I'm not one for the ceremonies.'

Beatrice nodded and glanced at the blank canvas on the floor.

'May we discuss the exhibition?' she asked.

'Sure.'

I pulled up two chairs, and Beatrice flipped open a steno pad where she was putting together her roster of paintings.

'Lucinda told me there are certain pieces you don't want to exhibit.'

'Right.' There was no question in my mind now. Lucinda was in communication with Schein, either directly or via her brother Leo. 'How many pieces are you going to need?'

'I normally look to exhibit twenty-five to thirty paintings for a single artist show. But since there are going to be three of you, I was thinking more like ten to fifteen from each of you, especially since the spaces I have in mind in both New York and Paris are fairly large.'

'In that case, I'll probably need to paint about three or four more pieces. We can use three of the ones you bought, *The Savior*, *La Santera*, and *Rio to Nowhere*. And I have four others here we might be able to use.'

'Not *Neglect*?'

'I'm afraid not, sorry.'

'What's that one?' Beatrice pointed at the covered board, which was on the floor propped against the wall.

'Something private.'

'Is it yours?'

'It's mine, yes. But it's not for display.'

'May I see it?'

She stepped over to the piece without waiting for a response and uncovered it. Then she stepped back, brought her hand to her mouth, and stared at it for a while.

'Put it up on an easel, please,' she whispered.

I lifted the piece off the floor and set it on an easel under one of the spotlights. I hadn't seen it since I'd finished it. It was like looking at someone else's work. I'd never felt that before. It took my breath away.

'It's magnificent,' Beatrice said. She reached out her hand and let it hover a couple of inches from the board. Then she swiveled around and stared at me, her eyes wide, her mouth slightly open.

'It's from the cockfight sketches you showed me.'

I nodded.

She looked back at the painting. 'But it's so much more than that now,' she said. 'This feather's amazing. The faces.' My heart raced as she stepped closer and peered at the painting. 'And this woman in the background; it's not easy to make her out.' She swung around. 'Is this your mother?' she asked in a lowered voice.

I looked around the room and nodded, bringing my finger to my lips and winking at her.

'Ah, I understand.'

I pointed out the image in the ceiling.

'Behold Changó the King.'

Beatrice examined that area of the painting.

'You'll be hearing more about him, I guess,' I said. 'Whenever you see a statue of Santa Barbara, the black Virgin with the blue robes, that's supposed to be him.'

Beatrice nodded.

'We absolutely must have this one for the exhibition,' she said. 'It's destined to be a standout. I have a good instinct for these things.'

I looked up again and saw Concha standing at the door to the open workspace. She was dressed almost identically to Beatrice, except for the heels. Concha was wearing dark sneakers and white bobby socks. She wriggled her fingers at me, and I waved her over.

'Someone's already bought it. Sorry.'

Beatrice pulled out a little notepad. 'Give me their name. I'll speak with them about borrowing it.'

'Hello, boyfriend.' Concha planted a wet kiss on my cheek. 'Hello, Beatrice,' she said without facing her. 'Hello, painting. Oh, wow.' She stepped back and stared at the painting with her lip-glossy mouth hanging open.

'Magnificent, isn't it?' Beatrice said.

Concha rolled her eyes and turned to me. 'When did you do this one?' She bowed at the painting. 'It has a strong energy.'

'I'd like to use it for the exhibition. But it's spoken for apparently.' Beatrice closed her notepad. 'Maybe you can convince the artist to speak with the new owner. Use your womanly powers of persuasion.'

Concha swung on Beatrice. Fake smile, teeth showing. 'Love the dig, girlfriend.' She sidled up next to me and grabbed my arm. 'What exhibition are we talking about?'

Beatrice put the notepad in her purse. The light had gone out of her face.

'Draw up a list of what you're willing to exhibit and another of what's left to paint. I'd appreciate accompanying sketches. Hand it all over to Lucinda by the end of the week. I'll be heading to Chicago next Monday to work out the selection with the artist from there. His name's Edward Jefferson. You'll like him.'

'You got it.'

Beatrice extended her hand, and I shook it. Then she turned on her heels to go.

'What exhibition is she talking about?' Concha asked.

I watched Beatrice cross the room. She halted just as she reached the entrance to the workspace and narrowed her eyes at the open doorway. A moment later she stepped back as Schein's driver entered the room and nodded a greeting at her.

'She's arranged an exhibition in New York and Paris with the center. They want to feature my work, along with a couple of other artists.'

Concha followed my line of sight and looked at Beatrice and the driver.

'What's that fucker doing here?' Concha punched me in the side. 'And when were you going to tell me about Paris?'

'You know him?'

Beatrice leaned against the wall, her arms crossed over her chest, and watched as Schein's driver walked toward us.

'We've had the pleasure, I'm afraid,' Concha said.

'I'm here to pick up the picture,' the driver said once he reached us. He tossed a sidelong glance at the painting. 'Is that the one?'

Concha stepped aside and looked at the floor.

'I'll pack it up for you.' I pointed back at the doorway. 'You can wait over there.'

'Don't worry about it. I can take it this way.'

'Wait over there while I pack it or come back another time. I'm not debating this.'

The driver wagged his head and walked away.

'That's telling him,' Concha said.

Beatrice's heels clicked against the wooden floor of the workspace as she marched back to us.

'You could have just told me it was my father who'd bought the painting.' Her words were tinged with a mix of anger and exasperation.

'Acquisitions are private. It's up to the buyer whether to make it public, not to the artist. You should know that.'

Beatrice glanced at the painting again and nodded.

'Let's speak soon.' She kissed me on the cheek and disappeared from the room.

'I warned you to steer clear of that shit,' Concha said, 'And what do you do? You go running to it like a dog to its own caca.'

'Shut up and help me with this.' I lifted the painting off the easel and headed for the packing room. 'We can talk about it over dinner if you're free.'

'Damned right, I'm free.' Concha followed close behind. 'This girl's fucking free as a bird, pendejo.'

18

Star-Crossed

'Mother fucker, hijo de puta, mierda for brains! How could you agree to that shit?' Concha flung an empty beer bottle into the viaduct. It exploded on contact with the concrete, some of the pieces making it into the flow of water in the center channel. It had rained recently, making the dead river come back to life temporarily.

'I had no choice.' I drained the last of my beer and cracked open another bottle. 'And I can't talk about it. So don't ask me anything else.' I handed her the bottle and opened another. 'In any case, it's not all bad. I'll be able to sell my paintings for more. Maybe even make it into one of those fancy-ass museums one day.'

Concha shook her head and reclined onto her back. She looked up at the moonless sky. The clouds had cleared, and the stars were standing out here and there.

'You're going to end up in bed with that *vieja*, I just know it. She's gunning for you. Then everything will turn to shit for you.'

'Not gonna happen, preciosa. She's not my type.'

Concha sat up. 'Since when does that matter? You think all the dudes I get with are my type?'

I set my beer bottle down hard on the ledge. 'It's not the same thing, Concha.'

'Don't kid yourself, mijo. That cunt's doing you a big favor. And it ain't for free. She's going to make you pay for it with your pee-pee.' She pressed her bottle against my crotch.

I laughed and took a swig of beer, then lit a cigarette and sucked on it, drawing the hot smoke into my lungs. I blew smoke rings at Concha, which she batted away.

'You're just jealous.' I kissed her on the cheek. 'I understand. But don't worry. Nobody will ever replace you. You're my *reina*.'

Concha rested her head on my shoulder.

'Your mother's your reina.'

'Okay, then you're my *princessa*.'

'And you're my *principe*.'

'We're royalty.'

'Like Jesus and La Magdalena.'

I lifted my head and looked at her. 'That's a weird comparison.'

'No, it's not. You're the Savior of 6th Street, and I'm your homegirl-*puta*. It's so Jesus and Mary Magdalene; it ain't even funny.'

I was feeling the effects of the seven beers, and my head was starting to spin. I didn't want to pass out again. So I pushed away the bottle, which was still three-fourths full, and rose to my feet, steadying myself against one of the iron spans.

Concha stood and wrapped her arms around my waist. She looked into my eyes, then touched her nose against mine.

'Mijo.'

'What?'

'Let me take you home.' She kissed me on the mouth. 'It's about time, don't you think?'

I shook my head. 'I don't want that for us. Things can't change that way.'

Concha closed her eyes. When she opened them again, they were full of tears. 'Then take me to Paris with you. I can protect you. Plus, we'll have fun parading up and down the Champs-Élysées, seeing the Eiffel Tower, going out to a real French cabaret, maybe take in a cancan show at the Moulin Rouge.'

I pulled out my bandana and wiped the tears from her face, which were now flowing down her cheeks. Then I kissed her on the forehead.

'We really are star-crossed lovers, aren't we?' Concha said.

'Maybe in a past life, Juliet,' I answered. 'Not in this one.'

* * *

Over the next few weeks, I skipped the gym and painted six hours a day, getting ready for the exhibition. I gave my academic counselor notice I'd be on hiatus from my studies the next semester as the tour would eat into my time. My only break was for Christmas, when the art center closed for the holidays, and I spent my time huddled over my sketchbook on the fire escape, on the bridge, in coffee shops, planning my repertoire.

By the time we were ready to ship the paintings to New York, I'd completed ten more canvases, including one of my father, baton in hand, making the Watts Towers rise from a field of landfill; one of Sexto and his grandmother ascended, locked in a phosphorescent embrace and surrounded by black storm clouds; and one that made people catch their breaths of my mother clad in a transparent sheath, rising from the sea like the Virgen del Cobre, with Beatrice sprouting Venus-like from her head. I called that one *Born Again*. Beatrice told me the blood drained from her father's face when he saw a photo of it. I frankly didn't care whether it made it into the show or not. It was reward enough to have been able to rattle Schein without violating the terms of our agreement.

Beatrice spent more of her free time with my mother, who had agreed to act as her sponsor for her year-long initiation into Santería, which would start once we got back from Europe. Beatrice had tried to convince my mother to let her buy us a condo on the Westside so she could be closer to her. But my mother steadfastly refused. Neither of us wanted to leave our apartment on 6th Street. So instead, Beatrice became a virtual third member of the family.

At first, I was weirded out by the whole thing and even tried to change Beatrice's mind, warning her about all the restrictions she would have to observe, including not touching anyone who wasn't a close family member and going around with a chaperone, like a child. I didn't see how she was going to be able to do any of it given her busy schedule. But she insisted it was what she wanted and started to dress in white, the color of a novitiate, and to drape herself in the colored beads my mother gave her. My mother assured me it was for the best now that I'd decided to join an exhibition funded by someone as dangerous as Schein. It was a way for her to keep an eye out for me through Beatrice who, unbeknownst to herself, would serve as a kind of spiritual listening device.

I saw a lot less of Concha in the lead-up to the exhibition. But whenever I bumped into her in the streets or at La Noche Buena, her joy at seeing me turned quickly into drama-filled scenes of crying and recriminations. As far as I knew, she wasn't aware of Beatrice's growing closeness with my mother, as that was an orbit that was foreign to Concha's. But she interpreted my lack of face-time as aloofness and felt hurt and rejected by it. The truth was that by the time I finished painting each day, I was exhausted and didn't feel much like going out. And no amount of reassurance made her feel any better. In the end, I suggested she hang out at the center where I was spending most of my time, which is precisely what she did from New Year's until we were ready to leave for New York in the spring. Every afternoon she would come to the art center dressed in jeans and a T-shirt and sit cross-legged on the floor, munching on bags of potato chips and staring at me while I painted. Afterward, we would grab a quick bite to eat, and she'd return home to do Lord knows what until the next afternoon when she'd return to watch me paint.

I felt caught between the proverbial rock and hard place, with Beatrice at home and Concha at the art center. And on the rare occasion when Beatrice would show up at the center to check on my progress, Concha would rear up, all claws and fangs, which killed my productivity for the rest of the afternoon.

'That chick is fucking weird,' Concha said to me one afternoon in late March after one of Beatrice's final visits to the art center before the tour. 'Who does she think she is dressing like some Caribbean goddess?'

I shrugged and started to put away my things. 'We're off next week, by the way.'

Concha wrapped herself around me, pinning my arms to my sides, my hands still grasping my paintbrushes. 'I'm going to miss you, mijo. I don't know how I'm going to be able to stand it.'

'I'll miss you too, preciosa.' I kissed her on the nose and wriggled out of her embrace. 'This is pretty much it now. I'll be busy with the final packing and stuff and will need to concentrate a hundred percent. So—'

Concha stepped away from me, her face contorting with a mix of frustration and anger. 'What are you saying? We're not going to see each other anymore?'

'Calm down, preciosa. I don't see how we can. I'm way too busy, and I rarely have enough time to sleep. I don't want to be exhausted at the start of the tour.'

'Take me with you. I can sit in a corner the way I do here. I promise I won't bother you.'

'I can't afford it, sorry.'

Tears streamed down Concha's face, streaking her mascara, and her voice was becoming increasingly hoarse. 'Please, Virgilio, please, it'll be perfect, New York and Paris in the spring. You and me. You and me, baby.'

I put aside my brushes and pulled Concha into an embrace, stroking her hair and kissing her cheeks and forehead. Lucinda was watching us from her office. She shook her head and closed the door.

'I promise, mija. When I get back, I'll have a lot more time. But this tour, it's going to be a lot of hard work, interviews, appearances—'

'Don't give me that shit. You're going to be living the high life, partying all the time. And one night, that vieja is going to sink her perfect bleached teeth into you and make you hers if she hasn't already.'

'There's nothing like that between us; I don't know how many times I have to tell you.' I kicked the easel, which shifted a couple of feet to the side and teetered, threatening to fall over. 'Goddamn it, Concha. Get a grip, or I swear, I won't be able to keep seeing you. I can't live like this. The stress is making a hell of my life.'

'Okay, I'm sorry! I'm just shocked it's our last night. It's kind of a bomb you dropped on me out of nowhere. You can understand that, right?'

I packed away my things in my locker while Concha watched. Then I secured the padlock and sped to the bathroom. Concha followed me inside, reclined against the wall, and watched as I washed my hands.

'Can I ask one teensy favor?' she said.

I dried my hands without saying anything and looked at her.

'Can we at least spend our last night together? We can go out and have dinner at a fancy restaurant; we'll have some champagne to celebrate your tour, and you can spend the night at my place. Like a real date.'

'I don't know about that last part.'

'It'll make things easier for me. I won't bother you again until you get back. I promise.'

We ended up at one of the restaurants in the Bonaventure Hotel, where Concha plied me with champagne and cocktails. Afterward, she dragged me to one of the hotel's passé discos, where we danced until the room was gyrating around me, and things started to go black.

The next morning I woke up in Concha's bed completely naked. Concha was passed out next to me, also naked. My chest went tight, and I felt a current of hot and cold surge into my face as the full realization of what had happened slammed me. It was obvious we'd had sex, of the wilder variety from the looks of it. After years of trying, Concha had finally gotten her way and had marked her territory. The problem was I didn't remember a goddamned fucking thing.

She was sitting up in bed in an emerald green nightie when I came out of the shower. She stretched her arms deliciously when she saw me, a look of bliss on her freshly made-up face, and greeted me with a wet kiss. I could smell a mix of alcohol and Binaca on her breath. My head was throbbing with the pain of a bad hangover.

'Ah, you can do better than that, loverboy.' She reached up and pulled my face toward her and kissed me again, this time on the mouth. 'Mmm, much better.'

She snatched at the towel I was wearing as I turned around to search for my underpants and pulled it off.'

'Hey!'

'Just stand right there where the sun's coming through the blinds. No, don't cover yourself. I want to see you naked in the clear light of day. That way whenever I miss you I can think of you like that.'

I shook my head and pulled on my underpants.

'What's wrong?'

'I've got a massive headache, sorry.' I cast about the room looking for my trousers.

'They're on this side.'

She pointed to a spot on the other side of the bed where I found them turned inside out. A couple of the buttons were missing.

'You're not rushing off, are you?' The smile was evaporating from her face. 'Let me make you some breakfast.'

I finished buttoning my shirt and sat on the edge of her bed, trying to think of something to say to mask my anger and disappointment in myself. I couldn't believe I'd let myself get into such an irreversible situation with her.

'I can't remember what happened last night, Concha. After the dancing.'

'What do you mean, silly?' Concha cocked her head and placed her hand on my leg. 'We came here. We made love.'

'I can see that. I just can't remember. It's all a blackout.'

She scooted closer and lowered her head to my lap.

'You seemed fine to me.'

'Did I?'

Concha sat up. Even I was surprised by the abruptness in my voice.

'Yes! You got it up perfectly fine. You even came two times.'

'Fuck me. I'm going to have to give up drinking.'

'Gee, thanks.'

I got up to put on my jacket and felt the room tilting, then I sat down and lowered my head into my hands for a moment, eyes closed.

'Maybe I *will* have that cup of coffee.'

'I'm sure it'll all come back to you eventually,' she said, breaking the silence as we sat across from each other at her breakfast table munching on buttered toast and sipping on our extra-strong cafés con leche.

'This is going to change our relationship, Concha.'

'I should hope so.'

'Not in the way you think.'

Concha set her lipstick-stained coffee cup down loudly. 'I'm not some naïve cunt, okay? I know you're not going to make an honest woman of me when you come back from Paris. But you're part of me now, in a way you never were before. And I hope it's not the last time. But if it is, at least we had last night.'

'You mean you had last night.'

Concha stood and started clearing the table. 'Well, then, next time maybe you should try it sober, mother fucker.'

She knocked into me as she passed on the way to the kitchen, and one of the cups fell to the floor and shattered.

'I'll get that,' she shouted as I bent down to pick up the pieces. 'Just go. If you have to go, just go.' She threw the rest of the dishes into the sink and ran into the bathroom, shutting the door behind her.

I finished picking up the remains of the cup and mopped the spilled coffee with one of her kitchen towels. Then I went to the bathroom door. I could hear Concha crying inside. Not her usual hysterical crying. This time it sounded different. More like when I found her sobbing behind the library when we were in high school, when she was still Jesús. The memory made me sad, and I felt a tightening in my throat.

I tapped on the door with the tips of my fingers and tested the knob. It was unlocked. I cracked open the door and poked my head inside. Concha was sitting on the edge of her bathtub crying. I sat next to her and rested my head on her shoulder, which seemed to calm her down.

'I didn't mean to be cruel, preciosa. I'm sorry.'

Concha kissed me on the head and put her arms around me the way she'd done countless times before. 'Thank you, mijo. Thank you for not just leaving.' She gently smoothened my eyebrows with a pass of her thumbs and flashed a sad smile. 'I love you, you know. I always have.'

'I know. I love you, too.'

'Then maybe it's not hopeless for us. We could be happy together. I'm sure of it. Maybe when you get back...'

19

New York

The gallery space Beatrice booked in New York was right on Fifth Avenue on the Upper East Side. I'd flown in a couple of days before the show. Beatrice had gone on ahead a day before me and was inside the gallery, directing the students from a nearby art college regarding the display when I arrived. She looked like an angel in her tight-fitting white blouse, flowing white skirt, and white open-toed heels. A white scarf covering her hair completed her ensemble of purity.

I was surprised to see Anne standing next to a podium at the end of the room, scribbling some notes in a steno pad. She was wearing a grey pinstriped pantsuit, black pumps, with her hair pinned up in the back, and a pair of black horned-rimmed glasses, looking like a female Clark Kent. She raised her eyes as I walked into the gallery and tracked my journey as I crossed the room and kissed her on both cheeks.

'There's a closet to hang your coat over there.' She pointed her pencil at one of several doors along the wall.

'I didn't know you were coming,' I said when I returned.

'Surprise. It seems you're wanted over there.'

I looked across the room and saw Beatrice waving me over.

'Are you following on to Paris?' I asked.

'I'm here for the whole of the tour. I'm covering it as part of a special feature for the *Herald.* So make sure you're on your best behavior.' A hint of a smile animated her otherwise deadpan expression.

'Maybe we can catch that drink after all,' I said.

'One never knows.'

Beatrice introduced me to the other two artists who had already arrived. There was twenty-five-year-old Miriam Blackfoot from near Seattle, a member of the Nooksack tribe who recorded life on her reservation on both massive canvases in mixed media and intricate woodcuts stained in natural colors. And there was Edward Jefferson, a shy twenty-year-old half black, half Chinese guy from Chicago whose impressionistic, almost idyllic portraits of gang life blew my mind. His acrylics made the horrific look as benignly inviting as a Norman Rockwell. We spent the next couple of hours admiring each other's work before heading back to the Midtown hotel where we were all staying.

Beatrice had arranged for everyone in our group to stay on the same floor. My room faced hers, which I found awkward, especially as I was hoping to connect with Anne, whose suite was further down the hall on my side. But Anne wasn't making things easy either, as I did my best to engineer an encounter in the hallway, the elevator, the lobby, the bar, or on my way to or from the restroom. Invariably, she found a way to evade me. But the cooler she played it, the more determined I was to hook up.

At dinner, despite my best efforts to snatch the seat next to Anne by practically pole-vaulting over two other diners, Miriam Blackfoot slipped into it ahead of me. I ended up sitting in the last available chair — the one next to Beatrice, who was dressed to perfection in a white, sequined Oscar de la Renta party dress topped off with a white turban. It took a massive dose of self-control and a tequila chaser to calm myself. But once the initial frustration dulled, I took a deep breath and decided to make the best of it, especially as Beatrice and I had a lot to chat about.

We spent most of the meal talking about the opening the next evening and the activities planned for the rest of the week. I noticed she was drinking juice instead of wine, presumably because of the Santería thing. As the waiters cleared away our dishes and the conversation around us died down, she smiled at me over the rim of her highball glass. The juice she'd been sipping had turned her lips, teeth, and tongue neon red, which made me smile.

'What is it?' she asked.

'Now, be honest.' I fingered her glass. 'Wouldn't you much rather be drinking a nice Cabernet?'

Beatrice glanced at her juice, then back at me. 'It's funny ... I don't miss it at all.'

'No?'

She shook her head and set down the glass. 'Not at all.' She glanced sidelong at the others, then leaned in and said in a lowered voice. 'It's like I've been reborn.'

'Really?'

She glanced down for a moment and drew a deep breath, then she raised her head and looked me straight in the eye. 'I know it sounds silly, Virgilio. But something's happening to me.' She held her palm over her chest. 'In here' — she touched her index finger to her forehead — 'and in here.'

I scooted closer to her and searched her face. 'You haven't even started your training, Beatrice.'

'I realize that. But what I've learned from your mother so far, and what I've experienced at the few meetings I've attended, I know this is what I need in my life. It's what I've been searching for...' Her voice trailed off as she watched the others getting up from the table and withdrawing to one of the several lounges.

'It's okay,' I said. 'You don't need to —'

'I've had this hole inside,' she continued, glancing to one side. 'Ever since I was a little girl. But that's all changing now…' When she looked back at me, her eyes were moist. 'I've grown so close to your mother, Virgilio. I feel loved and protected whenever I'm around her. You have no idea how lucky you are. I never had anything like that with my own mother. She was always so cold and distant.'

'I'm happy for you, Beatrice.' I stood and led her by the hand to one of the smaller lounges with a large crackling fireplace. We curled up on one of several dark velour couches and sipped hot drinks, an Irish coffee for me and hot chocolate for Beatrice. I noted a slight trembling of her body as she reclined against me and stared pensively into the fire. Gone was the confident woman I'd met a few months ago. She'd been replaced by vulnerability incarnate wrapped in white and on the verge of losing her shit. Responding to a sudden protective instinct, I pulled her close and rubbed her back with the palm of my hand. She relaxed into me and closed her eyes.

After a moment, she said, 'I've just been thinking about my father.'

The moment Beatrice mentioned Schein, a red alert went off in my head. I straightened up and put my cup on a side table, pushing it out of my reach. I had to make sure I didn't drink too much. It was critical that I maintain control of the situation and avoid even the remotest chance of this turning out like my last night with Concha.

'It's thanks to him that this tour even happened,' she said in a lowered voice.

'I sort of figured that.' I flagged down a waiter and asked for a glass of water.

'Ever since I returned from South Africa, he's always been so supportive of me, in a material sort of way.'

The waiter handed me a glass of water, which I drained in one gulp and handed back to him, asking him for another. Beatrice kept speaking on autopilot.

'I mean, he didn't have to, you know.' She looked at me with an intense look. 'He's a busy man, what with his part of the family's banking empire to direct and his development projects. There's no reason for him to take such an interest other than his love for me as a daughter, right?'

It was now clear to me that Beatrice had no idea about her father's criminal activities. To her, he was a successful banker and developer, plain and simple, who was rarely home due to his busy schedule. That said, I determined that I wasn't going to be the one to break the bad news to her.

'Absolutely,' I responded.

'Yes, absolutely. And, if I'm honest, any success I've had in my life has been largely due to him.'

'I doubt that's true, Beatrice.'

Beatrice waved her hand dismissively. 'Anyway, the point is, I've decided that the time has come for me to break free from him. To make my own way.' She glanced at me, her face serious, her forehead furrowed. 'Don't you think?'

'It's not really my business, to be honest.'

'I'm twenty-seven, Virgilio, for God's sake! It's time.' Beatrice drew herself up. 'It's thanks to your mother that I've found the strength inside to make that break.'

I looked at the crackling fire, taking a moment to think of the right response, something supportive but noncommittal. Unable to come up with anything, I looked back at her and punted. 'Like I said, I'm happy for you, Beatrice.'

Beatrice frowned, her eyebrows meeting in the middle. 'He won't let me go without a fight, Virgilio. It's all about control with him. It's always been that way. The irony is I've always felt a comfort in knowing he was controlling everything, you know, that he was taking care of all the details. And as long as my mother and I went along with what he wanted everything was okay. But if we didn't, if we ever stepped out of line ... oh, Lord.'

'What?'

Beatrice's eyes went wide, and she stared vacantly across the room. 'He has a temper, Virgilio. Real scary. As hot as a block of dry ice.' She stared at me. 'The fear of being on the receiving end of that temper kept me from ever feeling close to him. That same temper led him to track me down to that village and force me to watch as my uncle and his friends strung up poor Teko.'

Her voice broke when she uttered Teko's name, and she fell against me and sobbed quietly into my chest. I was beyond shocked at how vulnerable Beatrice had allowed herself to become with me and was at a loss as to how to react. So I stroked her back until her sobbing subsided. It was the best I could muster. At that, I caught sight of Anne in the mirror over the fireplace, glaring in our direction. As our eyes met, she shook her head and disappeared. I checked my watch and saw it was well past eleven.

After a few minutes, Beatrice sat up with a slightly embarrassed look on her face, and I offered her a glass of water from which she took a few halting sips. We tried to dispel the awkwardness by exchanging a few random comments about the show. But it was late, and we were both exhausted, and we all had to be up by eight the next morning. So we gradually made our way out of the lounge and up to our floor, where we kissed each other good night and withdrew into our respective rooms.

The telephone on my nightstand was ringing as I opened the door. I crossed the room to pick it up, but it stopped just as my fingers touched the receiver. I went to close the curtains and stood at the window for a while, looking at the view south over Times Square toward Brooklyn. There wasn't much to see at that time of night. After a moment, all I could see was my reflection in the glass, staring back at me. Stepping away from the window, I kicked off my shoes and unbuttoned my shirt. Then the telephone rang again.

'Where the fuck have you been? I've been calling you for over two hours.' It was Concha, and I could tell from the way she was slurring her words that she was drunk.

'Calm down, mija. I just got back from dinner.'

'It's fucking midnight over there, cabron. Don't lie to me.'

'Concha, listen to me. We're a big group of people here. There are artists, journalists, promoters—'

'She's there.'

'Of course she's here. It's her gig.'

'You'd better not get together with her, pendejo. Or, I swear, I'll sew her up so nobody can ever get with her again.'

'You're going to have to trust me on this, Concha. I promise nothing like that is going to happen.'

'Swear it to me.'

'Yes, I swear it.'

'On your mother's life.'

'Fuck you.'

'On your life then.'

'I swear on my life I won't get together with her, Concha. Not now; not ever. Now it's your turn. Swear to me you won't call me again while I'm on this trip. Because if you do, we're done. Understand? I love you, but I can't have you messing up this opportunity for me.'

The phone went silent for a moment. If it weren't for the faint sound of music from a transistor radio playing in the background, I would have concluded Concha had hung up.

'Well?' I said.

'I promise. I won't call you.'

'Swear it. On your life.'

'My life ain't worth nothing. It's a piece of garbage without you. Here today; in a dumpster tomorrow.'

'Swear it anyway.'

'Okay, loverboy. I swear on my piece of shit life I won't call you again while you're on your trip.'

An hour later, I was still trying to fall asleep. My thoughts were driving me mad. Concha was out of control, and I was afraid of what she would do to herself. Beatrice was an accident waiting to happen. And I felt pressed in the middle, with Schein's threat hanging over me if I misstepped. So I fished a dime bag out of my luggage and rolled a fresh joint, then sat cross-legged on the bed and smoked in the dark until all I was holding was a tiny roach. Then I closed my eyes and fantasized about Anne for a while, jerked off, and fell asleep.

* * *

Opening night was a success. Whatever Beatrice had done to promote the event to New York's art world glitterati had worked in a big way. The gallery was wall-to-wall people from the time we opened until the time we closed. And as Beatrice had predicted, the star of the show was my *Savior* portrait. By the end of the night, there were red dots on three-quarters of the entire collection.

The rest of the week was a firestorm of activity for us, including early-morning radio and television talk shows, visits to local elementary and high schools, interviews with local journalists, and a bit of touring in between. If I was lucky with the timing, I was able to fit in a quick swim or a workout in the hotel gym. After an early dinner, we would all cram into a couple of cabs and head back to the gallery for a few hours of face-time with the public. Then the evening was ours.

After the gallery, I preferred to head straight back to the hotel with the intention of doing some sketching or some reading if I was too tired. Usually, though, I ended up taking a walk with Beatrice, which would end with us holed up in a coffee shop where we would chat about anything and everything before retiring for the evening. But on our last night, I let the others convince me to go dancing at Studio 54, which wasn't far from where we were staying. Some anonymous person had arranged everything with the doorman for us, and we were all curious to experience the place, even in its decline. I was happy to find it was Latino night. The music was a mix of salsa, cha-cha-cha, and cumbia; the cocktails were tropical; and the crowd was a zoo of mainly gay guys strutting and posing in Hawaiian shirts, satin bellbottoms, and platform shoes. It was weird but fun.

At one point, I took a break from the dancing, leaving Beatrice on the floor to gyrate with the others, and headed to the bar to cool off over a drink or three out of sight of the others. As I caught my breath and mopped my forehead with a couple of cocktail napkins, Anne appeared at my side and touched a cold finger to my wrist.

'I'll have that drink now,' she said. 'A double vodka on the rocks would be perfect.'

'Oh, you like the hard stuff, do you?' I swiveled my stool to face her, and my eyes immediately went to the swell of her breasts, which were enhanced by a light-green low-cut blouse with tiny buttons that were begging to be undone.

'I'm up here,' she said, tapping a finger to her left eye.

My face went hot as I looked her in the eye. 'Sorry,' I said, 'I just—'

'Never mind about that.' She inclined her head toward the bartender who was moving toward us. 'My drink, please.'

We took our glasses to a private spot behind the bar and sat next to each other. I couldn't believe my luck. All week long, Anne had been avoiding any direct contact with me, preferring instead to watch me from a distance. At first, I felt like I was being spied on. But I didn't want to get paranoid as it would ruin the trip for me. So I'd made it a point to ignore her until, in time, she became part of the background noise. And now here she was sitting inches from me, making good work of her vodka, and regarding me over the top of her glasses.

'Is this where you interview me about the show?' I tossed back a tequila shot, chased it with a swig of beer, and flashed a Cheshire grin at her.

'I'm not working tonight.'

'Then what is this?' I asked.

'It's our last night in New York.'

'That it is.' I let my gaze drop to her blouse again for a moment and looked back up at her. This time she didn't flinch.

'You've done very well so far,' she said. 'You must be pleased.'

'You're talking about the show now?'

Anne nodded, drained the last of her vodka, and set the glass on the table. She held up a finger at a passing waiter and pointed at the glass.

'I'll have another double,' she said.

'Really?' I said as the waiter sauntered toward the bar.

Anne shook her hair and laughed. I was momentarily shocked. I'd never heard her laugh before. It seemed so out of character.

'Oh, now you're making me out to be a lush, are you?' she said. 'You're one to talk.'

'What do you mean?'

'Never mind.' She picked up the glass the waiter had just deposited on the table and took a long sip, closing her eyes and letting herself feel the cool drink run down her throat.

'What do you say we go back to the hotel and have our drinks there?' I said.

'In your room, I suppose?'

'Yours or mine. Doesn't matter to me.'

'Won't your girlfriend mind?'

'What girlfriend?'

Anne nodded at the dance floor. I could just make out Beatrice, participating in a line dance, her hands on the hips of the person in front of her.

'She's more of a big sister.' I looked back at Anne. 'It's not a problem.'

'Looks more intimate than that to me.'

'Things aren't always as they appear.' I reached over and took the glass out of her hand. 'We're close. But I have no interest in her that way.'

I stood and held out my hand. 'Shall we?'

Anne stared at me for a moment and allowed her eyes to do their own wandering. Then she took my hand and let me pull her up. We separately excused ourselves from the others and met at her room twenty minutes later where we had sex for nearly half the night. Anne was up for anything and everything, which took me by surprise, and we let our imaginations take us to incredibly pleasurable places I'd never been. It was the first time I'd ever made love with someone without any ground rules or boundaries.

The next morning, Anne woke me up for another round of intense lovemaking that lasted at least an hour, followed by a nice warm shower during which we soaped each other up and took full advantage of the lather before rinsing ourselves off and toweling each other dry.

I walked back into the bedroom to get dressed, leaving Anne in the bathroom to dry her hair. As I tied my shoes, I noticed a red light flashing on the telephone on her nightstand, indicating a voicemail message. The blow dryer was still humming in the bathroom, so I picked up the receiver and pressed the button to listen to the message. My chest went immediately tight on hearing the voice on the other end of the line. It was Leo, Schein's stooge, asking Anne to call him back.

'What are you doing, Virgilio?' Anne was staring at me from the bathroom doorway with her arms crossed.

'What are *you* doing?' I asked.

She narrowed her eyes and moved slowly toward me. I held out the receiver to her. She took it out of my hands and put her ear to it, and I pressed the repeat button. Anne listened to the message and put down the receiver.

'You want to explain that?' I pointed at the telephone.

'Not particularly.'

'You're working with them?'

'It's none of your business.'

'Fine. What about last night? And this morning?'

Anne shrugged. 'Best sex I've had in a long time. Thank you.'

She crossed the room to her closet, pulled out her suitcase, and put it on the bed.

'Checkout's in an hour. You'd better go back to your room and pack your things,' she said.

'I'm not leaving until I get an answer. What are you playing at?'

Anne crossed her arms again and glared at me with her head tilted up. She suddenly looked six feet tall.

'I told you to be on your best behavior. Now I've guaranteed that.'

'How so?'

'You've been cozy with Beatrice all week. People are talking.'

'I told you there's nothing between us.'

'For now, maybe. But it's only a matter of time before a horny boy like you in his sexual prime and a needy woman like Beatrice tick over into something more than confidantes.'

'For God's sake, Anne. She's your friend.'

'Which is exactly why she won't go there with you if she knows I was there first.'

'I'll tell her what happened.'

Anne laughed. 'Please do so. It'll save me the trouble. Now run along before you say or do anything stupid.'

My body was trembling with rage, and I held my fists clenched at my side. I stared into her eyes, which had become ugly and hard, and slowly released the breath I'd been holding for a few seconds.

'It's pure evil, what you've done,' I said.

'That's your reality. Not mine.'

'Evil never goes unpunished.'

'Oh, please, little boy. Look around; open your eyes.'

I moved toward her. She held up an open palm at me.

'Please leave before I call security and have you removed.'

We were standing nose to nose. I could smell the toothpaste on her breath. Anne held her ground.

'There are unseen forces in this world,' I whispered, 'that when unleashed are able to exact severe punishment on those they protect.'

'Silly boy.'

'This won't end well for anyone.'

'Stop talking, Virgilio. You're embarrassing yourself. Now turn around, march back to your room, and let's forget this ever happened. As long as you keep your distance from Beatrice, everything will be fine. I won't need to say anything to anyone. Maybe you'll even become a famous artist one day and put that sad little corner of the world you come from on the artistic map.'

'Simple as that?'

'Yes. Simple as that.'

I bumped into Beatrice as I came out of Anne's suite. It took a moment for her to register what she was seeing. Her face clouded over, and she put her head down and sped toward the elevators. I thought to follow her to explain everything. But I didn't know where to begin, and I didn't want to make matters worse by rambling something I hadn't thought through. So I left it for the moment and went to my room to pack.

20

Paris

Beatrice and I didn't exchange a word until after we reached Paris, when we unexpectedly found ourselves sharing a two-person elevator in the hotel where we were staying in the Marais the evening before our opening night. We were both late for the welcome dinner a local art academy was putting on in our honor at the Picasso Museum. Everyone else has gone on ahead. Beatrice looked close to tears, which contrasted with the festive colors she was wearing. I was startled and a bit sad to see she was no longer wearing white.

'Can we talk?' I asked.

'We *will* talk, Virgilio. Just not tonight. Not about that.'

I touched her hand. 'I'm sorry.'

Beatrice nodded and stepped out of the elevator as we reached the ground floor.

'You go on ahead,' I said. 'I'll catch up later.'

I watched as Beatrice exited the hotel and walked quickly in the direction of the museum, which was only a couple of blocks from where we were staying.

I stepped outside and looked up and down the small road at the gorgeous seventeenth-century architecture of the Marais. The twilight was burning out its last at the edge of the sky — electric blue tinged with a deep red. A few minutes more and it would be dark. I looked up and saw a few stars; the planet Mars was rising in the east. The weather was unseasonably warm, and I took in the scent of an unseen magnolia tree that was probably growing in a garden behind the walls of one of the ancient mansions dotted around this section of Paris.

A boisterous group of around fifteen college-age guys in blue blazers and white trousers jostled past me on the sidewalk headed in the opposite direction from the museum. A few of them were carrying guitars, a couple of others different sorts of percussion instruments. One of them, a tall black boy of around eighteen or nineteen who was bringing up the rear, turned and smiled at me just as they reached the corner and veered onto the main road. I chased after them and sidled up to the black boy. He didn't seem surprised by my sudden appearance, although the ones nearest him glanced at me with mild curiosity for a couple of seconds before they got used to my presence.

Between my sketchy knowledge of French and the little Spanish he knew, I found out from the black boy, whose name was Marcel and whose parents were immigrants from Benin, that the group was marching toward the Champ de Mars, a large public green space in the shadow of the Eiffel Tower, for the annual singing party sponsored by all the local colleges. The evening was warm, and the sidewalks were buzzing with people in a festive mood. After a couple of blocks, Marcel threw his arm around my shoulder and invited me to tag along. Someone from the front of the group tossed a cold can of beer in my direction, which I cracked open and shared with Marcel. This unexpected camaraderie was just what I needed after what had gone down in New York with Anne and Beatrice. I knew I'd have the devil to pay later for skipping dinner. But I pushed that out of my mind and promised to allow myself to live in the moment and unquestioningly follow wherever the circumstances of the evening led me regardless of the consequences.

We crossed a busy road, ran down some concrete steps to the banks of the Seine, and marched west toward the Eiffel Tower, which loomed in the distance. The guys chanted and sang, and I did my best to join in. Marcel and I traded breathless comments in an attempt to exchange bits of information about life in Paris and Los Angeles. He was curious about my black heritage, and about what it was like to be a child of immigrants in the United States compared to his experience in France. When he found out I was an artist and that I was going to be exhibiting in Paris, he surprised me with a brotherly kiss on the cheek, announced it to the others, and promised to come to the opening the next night.

I could hear singing in the distance as we neared the Eiffel Tower. Hundreds of voices chanted the *Marseillaise*, accompanied by rhythmic drumming. It went on and on as if on a loop. The group I was with took up the chant as we bounded up the steps to street level and jogged to the Champ de Mars, which was jammed with students from all over Paris. There were groups from all-boys schools, all-girls schools, mixed groups, each wearing the unique uniform of their particular school. There was even a group from the art school wearing nothing but paint on their bodies. We found a spot on the grass and collapsed onto it in a pile, using each others' bodies as chairs and pillows. I loved how demonstrative and tactile these people were with each other. Marcel and I rested our backs against one of his friends who was reclining on his stomach behind us, and we shared a filterless cigarette.

I lost count of how many beers I downed as we sang and chatted. But when I got up to stretch my legs, I felt them buckle under me as I experienced a dizzying head rush. I dropped to one knee and looked around. Since I'd skipped dinner, the alcohol had gone straight to my head. Everything was going black, and I could hear the flapping of bird wings in my head. A giant hand had reached into my chest and was squeezing my heart.

I reached out and felt Marcel's strong arms around me. He cleared an area on the grass and stretched me out on my back, passing his hand over my forehead, peering into my eyes, and telling me to breathe slowly and deeply. Someone else brought over a bottle from which I sipped a bit of tepid water. After a few minutes, I sat up and put my head between my legs. The singing was dying down. I looked up and saw the park had cleared out a bit. Marcel and his friends gathered around me; I reassured them I was feeling better and apologized for making a scene.

Marcel offered to walk back to the hotel with me. He stretched out his hand to help me to my feet, which made his blazer inch up his arm. I immediately noticed a multicolored beaded bracelet on his wrist. It was an amulet similar to the ones my mother wore.

'Where did you get that?' I tugged on his sleeve.

He shrugged and self-consciously pulled down his sleeve over the bracelet.

'You know Lucumí?' he asked, using the Yoruba word for Santería.

'My mother's an *Iyalawo*.'

Marcel backed away a little, and his eyes went wide.

'I knew it,' he said. 'I could feel it when we passed you. There's a strong current of aché flowing from you.' He pressed two fingers to my brow. 'Here' —he closed his eyes for a moment, then opened them and held the palm of his hand over the top of my head. '—and here.'

'It's more my mother's thing, to be honest.'

'Your orisha, it's Oshún, right?'

'Like I said—'

'I'm right, aren't I?' Marcel said. 'She's mine, too.'

I looked around. The vast park was now mostly empty. I felt exposed, practically naked, standing in the darkness with the massive iron structure of the Tour Eiffel towering over us.

Marcel took my hand. 'Come,' he said. 'Let's get you something to eat. Then I want you to accompany me somewhere.'

My first instinct was to resist. Now that the party was over and the reality was sinking in that I was in a foreign city in the company of a total stranger whose intentions I didn't entirely understand, friendly as he had been, I found myself craving the safety of my hotel room surrounded by people I knew.

'It's no coincidence we met.' Marcel grasped me by the shoulders. He looked me in the eye. 'Everything is meant to be. Close your eyes; look inside and follow me.'

When I opened my eyes a couple of minutes later, I saw Marcel standing under a street lamp at the edge of the park. The promise I'd made to myself to live in the moment ached at the back of my head. It drove me forward across the damp grass and brought me alongside Marcel who nodded and hailed a passing cab. He opened the door, ushered me into it, and followed me inside. Then he leaned forward and whispered an address in the ear of the cab driver.

'Where are we going?' I asked

Marcel sat back and patted my leg as the rickety cab sped away from the curb. 'You know Montmartre, Sacré-Coeur? The big white church on the hill?'

'We're going there?'

'Near there. A place called La Goutte d'Or in the 18th Arrondissement. It's an African neighborhood.'

'I thought we were getting something to eat. I'm starving. Plus, I don't feel well.'

'We can get something to eat there. It's not far, I swear. Come, put your head here. You can rest.' He indicated his lap, and I shook my head.

'Thanks, but no. I get sick if I close my eyes in a moving car.'

The city flew past the window as the cab roared down the relatively deserted street along the Seine and turned north and headed straight toward the illuminated white dome of Sacré-Coeur keeping watch over the illuminated city. Marcel explained that the neighborhood we were going to used to be white and working class and dull, but immigrants from north and west Africa had transformed it into a vibrant destination for all things African. Our cab climbed the hill, wound its way through the quaint streets of Montmartre, past iconic Sacré-Coeur, and descended on the other side into a deserted, shabbier version of the neighborhood we'd just driven through. It halted in front of a Beninoise restaurant. A plus-size, leathery black woman was standing in front of the restaurant dressed turban-to-sandals in white and awash in multicolored beaded necklaces.

'This is it.' Marcel grabbed my hand. 'You'll love it.'

The woman approached us as we climbed out of the cab.

'Welcome, welcome,' she said to me in heavily accented English. 'At last, you're here.'

I glanced at Marcel as he exchanged a few earnest words with her in a language I didn't understand. Then we followed her inside and sat at a table while she went into the kitchen to prepare something for us to eat. In the meantime, we munched on a few pieces of stale French bread and drank some hot greenish tea.

'What did she mean at last you're here?'

'She's Iyalawo, like your mother.' Marcel leaned toward me and whispered. 'Aché is very strong in her.'

The woman came out of the kitchen balancing a serving tray on one hand and holding a couple of bottles in the other. She placed them on the table and served each of us a bowl of steaming hot broth, a plate of stringy red meat with rice, and a basket of doughy beignets. Then she withdrew to the other side of the restaurant and watched us as we devoured our food. I could hear her humming a tune to herself. Every so often I looked up and smiled at her. She would respond the same way every time with a slow nod of her head. After a few minutes, I felt much better, reenergized in fact, wondering what was going to happen next.

I glanced at the wall clock. It was already midnight.

The woman cleared the table when we finished and disappeared into the kitchen.

'Thank you for that,' I said to Marcel, pulling out my wallet. He grasped my hand and shook his head.

'It's covered, brother.'

The woman came out of the kitchen carrying a newly lit cigar and stood at the table next to me.

'This was delicious, thank you,' I said.

'It's Beninoise,' she answered. 'Do you know it?'

'No, it's my first time. I hope it's not the last. I'm here for a week with some people from America. Maybe I can bring them one of these days.'

'My friend's a famous painter,' Marcel said in French. 'He's exhibiting in the Marais.'

'Follow me,' the woman responded. She moved to a dark doorway and passed through a beaded curtain. A moment later a dim yellowish light came on beyond the beads in what looked like a narrow passageway. I stood and moved toward it, then stopped and looked back at Marcel who was still sitting at the table.

'She meant you,' he said.

'Why me?'

Marcel stood and walked up to me. 'You still don't understand?' He placed his hand on my shoulder. 'It's no coincidence we met tonight.' He nodded at the doorway. 'Follow the Iyalawo.'

She was standing at the end of a long hallway waiting for me. I followed her downstairs and into a round, windowless room decorated in palm fronds covering the walls and ceilings. It had the feeling of a hut somewhere in the bush, not of a flat in the middle of the sophisticated French capital. The woman blew cigar smoke on me, fanned my head with some leafy branches, and chanted words in Lucumí to prepare me for a spiritual consultation not unlike the Dilogún I was used to back home in Los Angeles. She invited me to sit on a straw mat and sat opposite me bringing out a box of cowrie shells, which she used for her reading. After a few minutes, she looked up with widened eyes and blew another lungful of smoke at me before speaking.

'A guardian spirit brought you,' she said. 'But that spirit is not enough here, so far away from your home.'

'Enough for what?'

She held up her hand and closed her eyes for a moment. When she opened them again, I swear I saw flames reflected in them. Then came the sound of wings again. It was as if the room were filling with hundreds of bird. I cast about the room looking for the source of the sound.

'You're in danger, boy. Great danger. You're in need of powerful protection.'

'What kind of danger?'

'Danger to your life; danger to your soul. This is the reason the guardian brought you here. I will seal you. As long as you follow my instructions, you'll be safe from any harm. The protection will last for one cycle of the moon. You must get more when you are home.'

'Okay, fine, Iyalawo.'

'One more thing before I seal you.' The corners of her mouth turned down, and she leaned forward on her knees. 'Someone is going to die. But as long as you do as I say, it won't be you.'

My mouth went suddenly dry, and I felt my stomach climb into my chest. 'Who's going to die?'

'There's a soul in play among your people,' she said. 'It could be anyone's. But follow my instructions, and it won't be yours.'

She spent the next quarter of an hour placing amulets on my wrists and ankles, tied a black choker around my throat, and draped a short beaded necklace over my head. Then she reached into the space between us, grasped at the air, and held up a feather that seemed to suddenly materialize in her hand. At that moment the sound of flapping wings stopped. I took the feather from her and examined it. It was identical to the one I'd found on my nightstand.

'Where did you get this?'

'Keep it with you at all times. Oshún has commanded.'

I put the feather in my shirt pocket and took instruction from the woman. Until the danger was over, I was to become like an *Iyawó*, a betrothed of Oshún. I was never to remove the amulets or necklace, I was always to keep my head covered, and I was to avoid alcohol and sex. As long as I followed these basic rules, the woman promised Oshún would protect me from harm. She also assured me a single slip-up would nullify the protection and expose my soul.

After the meeting, I paid the woman and ran upstairs to find Marcel. But he was no longer there. I went outside and looked up and down the street. But I couldn't see him anywhere. I was exhausted to the point of collapsing and tried to wave down a cab. But the two that passed me were occupied. So I started back toward Sacré-Coeur on foot, as it was a landmark I could use to get my bearings. From there, I descended the steps and headed toward what I hoped was the right way to the Marais. I was finally able to hop a taxi in Pigalle across the street from the Moulin Rouge. Twenty minutes later, at two in the morning, I stumbled out of the cab and rang the doorbell to the hotel where we were staying and waited for the desk clerk to let me inside.

21

Resurrection

I woke up to the sound of the telephone ringing in my room. I glanced at the clock radio and saw it was almost noon. It was Beatrice calling. She was upset I'd missed the dinner, especially as our hosts had held it in our honor and were eager to meet me. But when I failed to show up for breakfast, she feared something terrible had happened. When I met her in the lobby a few minutes later, with my sketchbook in hand, her mouth dropped open at the sight of me.

'Why are you dressed like that?'

I saw my reflection in the wall mirror behind her. I looked strange even to myself. I'd found a white paisley bandana and wrapped it around my head, and was wearing a plain white dress shirt and jeans. I'd tucked the beads inside the shirt so as not to be too conspicuous. But I couldn't do much about the choker and bracelets, which shone up clearly against my skin. On top of that, I looked a bit scruffy, not having shaved in a couple of days, and there were dark circles under my eyes.

'I'll tell you at lunch. I'm starving.'

We bought a couple of baguette sandwiches and a bottle of sparkling apple juice and sat on a bench in the Place des Vosges to have a picnic. The square was magical at that time of day, with the surrounding buildings glowing red in the bright sunlight. We weren't due at the gallery for the gala opening until six that evening, so we still had some time yet before we had to go back to the hotel to get ready. I told Beatrice all about the night before, leaving out the bits about the feather and about someone dying. She was keen to learn all the details of the reading, comparing it with her own experience, notably as it was African rather than Afro-Caribbean. She still felt a close affinity to the continent and the people, and she made me promise to take her to meet the Iyalawo.

When we finished our lunch, we sat silently in the warmth of the square, looking at the families with their children and at little groups of tourists scattered about. Beatrice seemed relaxed on the surface, but there was a sad look in her eyes, which were shining in the afternoon light. I opened my sketchbook and started to outline her face. She reached out and tapped her fingers against the sketchbook.

'Not now, Virgilio. We have to talk.'

I set aside the sketchbook and drew my feet onto the bench.

'When I saw you coming out of Anne's room the other morning—'

'You never let me explain about that.'

'There's nothing to explain. You're a young man, and she's an attractive woman. Things like that are bound to happen. To be honest, I have more of a problem with Anne than with you. She should have known better. What I wanted to say was that the incident forced me to examine my feelings for you.'

'What feelings?'

'I felt hurt when I saw you. And I became angry because I didn't know where the pain was coming from. Was it jealousy, a feeling of betrayal, shock? I was still processing it all last night when we were on our way to dinner. But when you didn't show up, and when I didn't see you at breakfast this morning, it finally dawned on me that the source of my feelings was my belief that you and I had developed a strong bond over the past few months, something I've never felt with anyone else before.

And it had nothing to do with my association with your mother.'

Beatrice's eyes were filling with tears. She looked away from me for a moment and dabbed at her eyes with a tissue she pulled out of her purse.

'Beatrice—'

'No, wait. I'm almost finished.' She set aside the tissue and looked into my eyes. 'I understand now I felt hurt because somehow I got it into my head there were no secrets between us. But that was shattered when I saw you coming out of Anne's room.'

I sat back on the bench. 'Beatrice...I hate to break it to you, but you don't know me at all.'

The corners of her mouth turned down the moment the words came out of my mouth.

'How can you say that?'

'Don't get me wrong. I feel close to you, too; closer than I've ever felt to anyone in a long time. But there's a lot you don't know about me. A lot.'

'In the sense that one can never thoroughly know someone else, I understand.'

'No. In the sense that there's a shitload of personal stuff I will never share with anyone except through my paintings. It's all there. If you want to know me, get to know my paintings.'

'I see.'

I scooted closer to Beatrice, who was retreating into ice queen mode.

'I'm sure that in time I'll feel comfortable enough to open up more with you. In the meantime, though, I was serious when I said I've never felt closer to anyone than I've felt to you in these last few months. That's something special, don't you think?'

* * *

The opening was meant to be a black tie affair. But I couldn't bring myself to put on anything as plain as a tuxedo. So I showed up at the gallery wearing an outfit I'd been planning ever since I was in Los Angeles. White shirt, white vest, white dress trousers, white espadrilles, and a white beret. The crowd of French sophistos parted for me as I walked through the door, like the Red Sea parting before Moses, and all conversation died down to scattered whispers. I took my place at the front of the gallery next to Beatrice and my fellow artists.

As soon as I settled in, a glass of soda in my hand, the master of ceremonies, a ruddy-faced gentleman in black tails and a white tie, welcomed the crowd in both French and English. He launched into a speech about the importance of inner-city art programs and the pool of incredible talent to be discovered in even the most deprived of places. He concluded by introducing each of us, the three American artists and the three French artists, saying something about our respective themes and the mediums we worked in. When he finished, he handed the microphone to Beatrice, who thanked the foundation in French for honoring her group of artists by inviting them to exhibit alongside the French artists. I hadn't expected it, but I never felt prouder and more humbled than in that moment.

I spent the remainder of the evening hovering near my section of the gallery, fielding questions from visitors about anything and everything they could think of, about the paintings, about my life, about America, Cuba, Mexico. I received invitations to dinner from interested women and even from a couple of men. I was interviewed for a French news channel and photographed. At one point in the evening, an older man in his seventies cornered me and spoke nonstop about the government's inadequate funding of art in cities outside the French capital. As I was trying to think of a way to gracefully bring the conversation to a close, I caught sight of Marcel holding a glass of wine and smiling at me. I raised my hand and excused myself from the gentleman, who pressed a business card into my palm as I disengaged from the conversation.

I hugged Marcel, who congratulated me and apologized for leaving me at the restaurant the night before. The truth was I hadn't given a thought to it and was just happy to see him again. He was curious about my paintings and asked me to tell him something about each one of them. Besides *The Savior*, which was everyone's favorite, the one he liked most was my mad portrait of Beatrice titled *La Enojada*. The combination of anger and sweetness, power and vulnerability that radiated from the subject moved him; he loved the way she anchored the center point of the painting around which whirled a tornado composed of random numbers and letters applied in a Pointillist style. Even after I finished answering his questions about my inspiration for the painting and the techniques I'd used, he continued to stare at it.

'Those eyes, they're extraordinary.' He stepped closer to the painting and peered at it. 'How did you decide on the color?'

I stepped to one side and spotted Beatrice across the room standing near the doorway of the gallery. She seemed to have wrapped up an interview of some kind. I smiled at her and waved her over.

'You'll get to see for yourself,' I said to Marcel.

He looked at me with questioning eyes as Beatrice crossed the floor. Her smile evaporated when she turned into my section of the exhibit and laid eyes on Marcel.

'Beatrice, I'd like to introduce you to my new friend Marcel. Marcel, this is my sort-of big sister Beatrice, La Enojada. As you can see' — I indicated her eyes with a nod of my head — 'they're violet, just like in the painting.'

Marcel beamed at Beatrice, who I could tell was at the point of tears. I excused myself from Marcel and pulled Beatrice aside.

'That boy,' she said. 'He looks exactly like Teko, the boy from South Africa. The one my father...' She was trembling, and I was afraid she was going to collapse. I escorted her to a chair and brought her some water, which she sipped, looking up every now and again at Marcel, who was staring at us.

'Who is he?' Beatrice asked.

'He's the student I met last night; the one who took me to see the Iyalawo.'

'He's Teko, Virgilio.'

'Beatrice, please. That's impossible. Teko was ten years ago. Marcel's only nineteen. He would have been nine years old then.'

Anger flashed in Beatrice's tear-filled eyes. 'I don't know how, Virgilio. But that boy is Teko.'

I looked back and forth between Beatrice and Marcel, who were staring at each other. Beatrice was gripping the sides of her chair to the point that her fingers were turning white from the pressure. I'd never found myself in such a crazy situation as this one. But I felt responsible for solving it, as I was the point of connection between the two of them. And I didn't think it wise to keep dissing Beatrice's insistence that Marcel was Teko. After all, who was I to know anything?

'Maybe you should talk to him.' I said.

Beatrice's head snapped in my direction. 'Talk to him?'

'If that is Teko, then you need to talk to him. Get the closure you never got all those years ago.'

Beatrice stared into the middle distance for a few moments. Then she refocused her eyes on me, took a sip of water, and nodded her head.

I went to Marcel and explained Beatrice's reaction by telling him he reminded her of someone from her past and that she wanted to talk to him about it. Marcel shrugged and followed me to where Beatrice was sitting.

'I'll leave the two of you to talk if it's okay. I'm heading back to the hotel.'

I kissed Beatrice and hugged Marcel, promising to give him a call in the next couple of days. Then I said my goodbyes to everyone on my way out the door and stepped out into the warm evening.

I walked back to the hotel feeling pretty well shell-shocked by what I'd just experienced and wondering what Beatrice was telling Marcel. An hour later I was pulling on my pyjamas getting ready for bed when I heard a pounding on my hotel room door. It was Beatrice. She slipped into my room, a troubled look on her face, and sat down on the ottoman. She refused the glass of water I offered her, and I sat on the bed across from her.

'What did he say?'

Beatrice shook her head. 'Sweet boy. I told him everything. But he didn't remember.'

'So it isn't him.'

Beatrice looked up at me. 'It's him, Virgilio. I'm telling you. There were a couple of things I told him that nobody else would have known that surprised him, that made him consider the possibility.'

'What things?'

'Things like the palm-sized birthmark on his flank; that he's flat-footed.'

A hot flush coursed through my body, and I felt suddenly short of breath. I stuck my hand into the pocket of my pyjamas and touched the feather the Iyalawo had given me.

'He agreed to take me to the woman tomorrow for a consultation. He said she would know if it's true.'

'What if she says no, Beatrice, that he's not Teko?'

'Then she says no. But now that I've found him, or someone exactly like him, I'm not going to lose him again.'

'What the heck does that mean?'

Beatrice sat on the bed next to me and took my hands in hers. 'I'm taking him back with me to LA.'

I pulled my hands away. 'That's crazy, Beatrice. You know that.'

'I'm not losing him again, Virgilio. This is my chance to make things right. I don't know how, and I don't know why, but this can't be a coincidence.'

'Assuming you can even do that, which I don't know you legally can, what's the guy supposed to do? Live with you? He's fricking nineteen.'

'He'll transfer to a university near me. He still has three years to go. Once he's finished, we'll see. He'll have a better life there than he does here.'

I jumped up from the bed, my fear ticking over into anger.

'You can't just move people around as if they were pieces on a chessboard, Beatrice. And how can you assume he'll have a better life in LA than in Paris? This is his home. His family's here. His friends are here. What you're offering him is culture shock and homesickness.'

Beatrice shook her head and patted the bed. 'Sit, Virgilio, please. Don't be upset. I'm feeling very vulnerable and confused at the moment. I need compassion, some warmth, not an angry lecture.' Her words were cut short by a sudden flood of tears. She reached out for the water glass, which I pressed into her hand. Then I sat on the bed, feeling terrible for making her cry.

'I'm so sorry, Beatrice.' I held her hands and kissed them. 'What do you say we talk about it in the morning when we're both fresher? If you want, I'll go with you to your consultation.'

She nodded and wiped her face dry with a tissue I handed her.

'And promise me you'll consult with my mother before you make any decisions. Since she's the one who's sponsoring your initiation, you should run anything like this by her.'

We talked some more about random things having to do with the exhibition and the activities planned over the next few days. But it felt forced. And we were both flagging, barely able to keep our eyes open. Finally, when it felt like the right moment, I stood and glanced at the door.

'May I stay here tonight, Virgilio?'

'Here?'

'I'd rather not be alone.'

I looked around the room searching for a guest cot I could sleep on.

'I can sleep on the ottoman,' she said.

'No way. It's too uncomfortable. You take the bed.'

'I can't make you sleep on the ottoman in your own room. Let's both sleep on the bed. There's space for the two of us.'

I looked at the bed, then at Beatrice, who was stretching and suppressing a yawn.

'I'm not so sure it's a good idea,' I said.

'It'll be fine.'

I took a deep breath, dimmed the lights, and slipped under the covers. She scooted over to me and held me close; her breasts pressed up against my chest. Her hair smelled faintly of an herbal shampoo. She was trembling, and I passed my hand along her back to soothe her. She buried her head against my shoulder, and a couple of minutes later she was dead asleep.

I waited a bit before I let go of her and rolled over onto my side, staring into the darkness of the room. I conjured up the image of my mother as I was suddenly missing her and feeling an aching in my chest. I imagined her standing watch over me in the middle of the room, a ghostly image, ethereal and softly glowing, a lit cigar in her hand. She looked at Beatrice and pivoted her head from side to side, signaling her disapproval. Then she puffed on her cigar, nodded at the ottoman, and blew smoke at it enveloping it in a protective cloud before vanishing. Taking her meaning on board, I crawled out of bed, careful not to wake Beatrice, and curled up on the ottoman, pulling a spare blanket over myself.

I awoke to the sound of the telephone ringing on my nightstand. I leaped from the ottoman and grabbed it. Beatrice opened her eyes and stared groggily at the digital clock. It was eight in the morning.

'There's a lady here to see you, Monsieur Santos,' the voice on the other end of the line said. 'I tried to stop her, but she's already on her way up to your room.'

'What lady?'

'An American black lady, monsieur. She seemed very agitated. Shall I call security?'

'Did she tell you her name?'

'No, monsieur.'

'Call security. Have them stand by.'

'Virgilio, what is it?' Beatrice was sitting up in bed.

'Trouble, I think. Maybe you'd better wait inside there.' I nodded at the bathroom, then grabbed a bathrobe and wrapped myself in it.

We were both startled by a pounding at the door. Beatrice slipped out of bed, ran to the bathroom, and pushed the door to, leaving it open a crack. The pounding continued until I opened it and found myself suddenly face-to-face with Concha, her face beaming with excitement. She was wearing a blue strapless summer dress and a black beret, carrying a white gift box in one hand, and grasping the handle of a roll-on suitcase with the other.

'Surprise!' She held out the box to me. 'And congratulations, mijo. I'm so sorry I couldn't make it last night to your opening. I tried hard to get a flight. But the only one they had was this damned red-eye. I'm so happy to see you.'

I took the box from her and stepped into the hall. She threw her arms around me and squeezed me, kissing my face again and again.

'I missed you so much, I thought I was going to die,' she said.

'What are you doing here, Concha? You promised to wait until after the show when I got back to LA.'

Concha let go of me and stepped back. 'No, I promised not to call you, and I haven't, have I? What I didn't promise was that I wouldn't join you for the last part of your trip, which is what I'm doing.' She looked down at herself and back at me. 'Aren't you even going to ask me inside so I can freshen up after my long flight to see you?'

I glanced over my shoulder at the door and back at Concha. 'Wait for me downstairs, please. I'll be right down, and we can have breakfast.'

'You're shitting me, right?' She tried to push past me toward the door, but I blocked her way.

'Who's in there, cabron?'

'Don't make a scene, mija. I'll explain everything over breakfast.'

'It'd better not be her, cabron. Or I'll fucking kill you both.'

She pushed past me, burst into the room, and found herself facing off with Beatrice, who was standing her ground next to the bed, arms akimbo. She was wearing one of the hotel bathrobes.

'Is there a problem?' Beatrice said. Her voice was calm and steady.

'The problem is you sleeping with my boyfriend.' Concha stepped up to Beatrice poking her finger at the air.

'Concha—'

Concha whirled on me. 'Shut up, motherfucker. You promised me.'

'I'm not sleeping with him. But if I were, I wasn't made aware there was a claim on him.' Beatrice directed this comment at me, an accusatory tone in her voice.

Concha lunged at Beatrice knocking her onto the bed. I leaped across the room, but by the time I got there, Concha was straddling Beatrice and grabbing her hair. It all happened so fast. She was screaming terrible insults into her face, and Beatrice was struggling to break free. A couple of hotel security guards exploded into the room, and between the three of us, we were able to pull Concha off Beatrice and restrain her.

'Motherfucker,' she screamed, struggling against the guards. 'Motherfucker. You promised me; you promised.'

'Calm down, Concha! Nothing happened. We were just talking.'

'Don't lie to me. She's fucking standing there in a nightie next to your bed.

'What's this about a promise, Virgilio?' Beatrice's voice was hard now, laced with anger.

'You shut up!' Concha screamed at Beatrice. 'Everything was fine until you showed up. If your daddy could only see you now.'

'Concha!'

Concha's head snapped in my direction. A new fire had ignited in her eye.

'Get her out of here,' I said to the guards. 'Now!'

Beatrice stepped forward. 'Excuse me?'

Concha swung on Beatrice, baring her teeth in a Doberman snarl. 'Mr. Maurice would be so proud of his little girl, shacking up with one of her artists, a black kid from the barrio ten years younger than her.'

'How do you know my father?'

'I said get her out of here.' I pushed at the guards, trying to get them out of the room. Just outside the door, a few hotel guests were milling about, trying to steal a peek at what was happening over their shoulders. There was the faint wail of a siren in the distance.

'No, wait.' Beatrice stepped up to Concha. There was suddenly an imperious air about her. And, for an instant, everything fell silent. 'I asked you how you know my father.'

'Everyone knows your father down where we live,' Concha spat out. 'And that albino of a driver of his, he's one of my most loyal customers; the freakiest, if you know what I mean. Just ask him.' She lifted her head at me. '*He* can tell you all about your father and all the shit he's into.'

Beatrice blinked at Concha, who had finally shut up, waiting for her words to hit their mark. At that moment, Anne poked her head through the door. Seeing what was happening, she pushed past the guards, stepped into the room, and took in the scene. Looking first at Beatrice in the bathrobe, then at me, her face reddened. Behind her followed three uniformed police officers, who exchanged a few words with the security guards. They promised to send someone to take statements and proceeded to forcibly remove Concha from the room. Her screams echoed off the walls of the hallway and the stairwell as they dragged her out of the building.

Anne, Beatrice and I stared at each other in the sudden stillness broken only by the receding siren of the squad car taking Concha away.

'It's not how it looks,' I said to Anne, finally breaking the silence.

Beatrice looked at me. 'What's this? Another promise?'

Anne turned on her heels and exited the room. I closed the door behind her. When I turned back around, Beatrice was still staring at me.

'What did she mean about my father?'

'You honestly don't know?'

Beatrice shook her head and sat on the bed, her expression softening. She reached for a glass on the nightstand. Finding it empty, she let it drop from her fingers to the carpet.

'That woman is mad,' she said.

'Before I left, I had sex with her. It was never that way with us before; it was the first time. Anyway, I promised her I wouldn't sleep with you.'

'I see.'

'Don't press charges against her, okay?'

'Why shouldn't I? The woman physically attacked me.'

'I just can't see her locked up in a French jail. Not the way she is, if you know what I mean.'

'She should have considered that before she assaulted me.'

I sat next to her on the bed and put my head in my hands.

'Tell me about my father,' she said.

I moved away from her. 'It's not my place to tell, Beatrice. You're going to have to ask him yourself.'

Beatrice rose from the bed and looked down at me. 'How long have you known, Virgilio?'

'You'd better get dressed. We have a long day ahead, and only an hour left for breakfast.'

'I'm disappointed, Virgilio. I thought we were friends.'

'Don't you even try to guilt me into telling you, because I'm not saying anything. I'm sorry, but there's a lot more at stake than our friendship. If you want to know, you'll have to ask him yourself. Or you can keep playing the ostrich. It's up to you.'

'What's that supposed to mean?'

I grabbed Beatrice's evening gown, and pressed it into her arms. 'I can't say anything more, Beatrice. Please...' She blinked at me for a moment and retreated slowly toward the door, looking a bit lost. My chest ached; a calloused hand was crushing my heart again. I wanted to run after her and comfort her, explain it all away and make things better. But I knew I would only make matters worse.

'I'll see you tonight at the gallery.'

'You're not coming to see the woman with Marcel and me?'

I shook my head. 'You can tell me all about it tonight.'

22

Crucifixion

The second night at the gallery was much more casual than the first and not as well attended. After spending most of the day being shuttled around Paris by a French escort who drove the other artists and me to our various appointments at schools, art centers, and a couple of local radio stations, I'd taken an extra-long nap in preparation for the show and had arrived a few minutes late.

At one point during the day, I managed to get a call through to the police station to ask about Concha and was told they'd be releasing her at eight o'clock the next morning due to a lack of evidence unless someone came forward to press charges in the next few hours. I promised myself to be there when she was released, then pushed it out of my mind to focus on the show.

I was surprised to see Beatrice wasn't there. Spotting Anne across the room speaking with one of the French artists, I walked over to her and waited to one side. When they finished, I asked if she'd seen Beatrice. She responded by walking away.

I strolled back to my section of the gallery and engaged in conversation with a few random visitors, all the while keeping an eye out for Beatrice. As the evening wound down, two men in dark trousers and white Polo shirts walked into the gallery. It was a uniform I immediately recognized. I reached into my pocket and fingered the soft feather buried deep inside. The men exchanged a look with Anne, who was standing by the door, and she nodded in my direction.

I stepped forward as they moved toward me.

'What do you want?' I asked.

'Don't make a scene,' one of them said. 'You're needed back home. We're here to make sure you get there.'

'I suppose you've already packed my bags for me.'

'Everything's in the van.'

'Hang on a second.'

I walked over to Anne, who was speaking with one of the French artists and pulled her over to one side.

'What's going on?' I asked.

Anne held up her hand at the men, who had started after me. They nodded and exited the gallery, waiting outside the door on the sidewalk.

'You know very well what's going on,' Anne said. 'You were warned multiple times not to get involved with Beatrice, including by me. You were told what would happen if you ignored those warnings.'

'When did I ignore them?'

'Last night, of course.'

'Nothing happened between us. She was upset about something and came to see me — as a friend. She ended up spending the night. But nothing happened. I slept on the ottoman, for fuck's sake.'

'You can explain it all to the people in LA. I'm done with it.' She turned her back on me and walked away.

A few minutes later, I found myself in the back seat of a van with darkened windows, being whisked away at high speed through the streets of Paris on our way to the airport. I didn't see any point in attempting an escape, and I was tired of the drama and tension I'd been exposed to since the start of the tour. So I chose instead to see the misunderstanding as a blessing in disguise, confident I'd be able to talk my way out of it once I was able to say my peace. My only worry was for Concha. But since I knew the police would be releasing her the next day, I felt sure she'd be fine and would be able to make her way back to the States on her own.

I filled an entire sketchbook between Paris and LA with comic book-style drawings of everything that had happened since we'd left Los Angeles over fourteen days ago. It was a cleverly disguised visual diary I hoped would come in handy when it came time to explain my side of the story. At one point when we were sitting in the airport waiting for our flight, one of the Polo-shirted guys paged through it, then shrugged and tossed it back. I took advantage of their disinterest and scribbled out a note asking for help and giving directions to where I was sure they were taking me.

A couple of hours before our descent into LA, I closed my eyes. The next thing I knew, my two escorts were hustling me out of the plane. I was still waking up when I stepped up to the immigration officer. Even though it had been their intention to approach the cubicle in one group, the attending officer insisted we come up one at a time. So my escorts ordered me to go first and whispered a warning not to try anything funny.

I handed the officer my passport, my customs declaration, and the note. My heart was hammering in my chest, and I could feel droplets of cold sweat trickling out from under my cap. I forced a smile to camouflage the tension I was experiencing.

'Remove the hat, sir.' The officer raised my passport and compared it to my face, then swiped it through a machine and typed a few things before snatching up the customs declaration. He didn't notice the note floating to the floor inside his cubicle.

'Anything to declare, sir?'

'Yes.'

The officer peered at the customs declaration, turned it over and narrowed his eyes at me.

'It says here you have nothing to declare.'

I glanced at my escorts, who were staring at me with hard eyes. I lifted my hand at them and smiled and looked back at the officer.

'My mistake, sorry.'

'What was that all about back there?' one of the Polo guys asked me when we were speeding down the hall to the baggage return area.

'Chill out, man,' I said. 'This isn't exactly the most normal situation for me. I was just nervous.'

A black car with darkened windows was waiting for us when we exited the international terminal, and we piled inside. This time I was pressed between my escorts, both of whom smelled of Fahrenheit and musk. As the car pulled away from the curb, one of them put his arm around me in an almost protective gesture, and I rested my head against his chest. I could hear the beating of his heart, the steady rise and fall of his breathing, the vibration of his voice as he exchanged comments with his counterpart. It was a struggle to keep my eyes open. So I closed them and half-consciously tracked our progress down Century Boulevard, onto the San Diego Freeway heading north, and south on the Santa Monica Freeway toward downtown.

It was dark when the car lurched to a stop next to the access point to the tunnels. The escort who I'd used as a pillow opened the door and waited for me to get out. He removed his sunglasses and stuffed them into the pocket of his trousers. The glare of a streetlight cut across his face. He was staring at me with a cruel, leering expression, one side of his mouth pulled back into a half-smile exposing half his teeth. Short, dark blonde hair, brown eyes, clean-shaven, angular face, slightly crooked nose, in his late twenties. He grasped me by both arms and turned me to face the access door, put both his hands on my waist, and moved me toward it. His counterpart faded into the background. I had the feeling I'd been claimed.

We dropped into the deserted central tunnel and walked past the flickering barrels, past the first couple of side tunnels. Our footsteps echoed off the concrete walls. It was the first time I'd ever seen the place devoid of people; it was usually vibrating with activity by this time.

'Where is everyone?' I asked.

'We're liquidating soon.'

My escort pulled up in front of a small access tunnel we had to crouch down to get into. He made me go first. When I was able to stand on the other side, I found myself in a dimly lit chamber with a dozen stall-like structures, each accessed by a half door. Another man stood in the shadows, holding what I assumed was a weapon. I wondered if this was the place where they'd kept Sexto prisoner.

My escort led me by the arm to one of the cubicles, opened the door, and waited until I went inside. There was a single cot, a small wooden table, and a flimsy plywood freestanding closet. He closed the door behind us.

'Am I allowed a phone call?' I asked.

'Who would you call if you were?' Now that we were alone, my escort's voice had taken on an odd, intimate tone.

'My mother, for starters. She's probably sick from worrying. She hasn't heard from me in a couple of days.'

My escort nodded and glanced around the stall for a moment before looking back at me. His eye fell on the choker the iyalawo had tied around my neck. He touched his finger to it.

'What are they going to do to me?' I asked.

'Depends on what you did.' He unbuttoned the top button of my shirt, and I held my ground, not wanting to appear intimidated, but shitting my pants about what the guy had in mind.

'I didn't do anything.'

'Then you have nothing to worry about.' He finished unbuttoning my shirt and pulled it open.

I removed my shirt and tossed it on the bed. 'You like tattoos?'

He stared at the sacred heart inked onto my chest for a few seconds, his mouth hanging slightly open, and looked up at me. I reached out and grabbed his hand and pulled it palm-open against my chest. His hand was cold. I searched my memories for the right incantation, something my mother used to say when I was a young boy, words in Lucumí that promised protection. I widened my eyes, leaned forward, pursed my lips, and waited. Then the words came rapid-fire, chanted below the range of human hearing. The stall filled with the sound of a thousand flapping wings.

My escort pulled his hand away from my chest and retreated a couple of steps. He cast around the room, then looked at me, blinking back the terror in his eyes. I calmly pulled my shirt back on, felt inside my pocket and touched the feather. Then the room fell silent again.

'What the fuck was that?' my escort asked.

'Let's just get this over with.' I pointed at the door. 'Go tell your boss I'm here.'

* * *

I waited about two hours in my stall before hearing anything from the other side of the door. There was a pack of cigarettes on the table and a book of matches I helped myself to. Then I paged through my sketchbook and recalled the events of the last couple of weeks again. I wondered if the immigration officer at the airport had ever found my note, or if a janitor had swept it into the garbage. And if he *had* found the note, I wondered if he'd turned it over to his supervisor or merely tossed it into a wastepaper basket.

The reflected sound of heavy footsteps approaching broke the stillness. Moments later, my escort, along with two other Polo-shirted guys, was marching me back to the central tunnel. We turned left past Molly's, which was dark, and into another side chamber I recognized as being adjacent to Leo's office. I was surprised to be pushed past his door to an opening in the concrete floor where we descended concrete stairs to a lower level. Firelight reflected in the stairwell from below. We emerged into a long narrow room with a high ceiling and a rounded end I figured was destined to be an employee meeting room of some kind. It reminded me of the interior of a pre-Christian Roman basilica I'd seen in a textbook for one of my art history courses. Torches had been installed all along the walls to the back of the room where there was a raised platform framed by what looked like a proscenium arch, and behind that, a chain link fence covered the back wall.

My escort pulled me by the arm, stood me in front of the platform and disappeared behind the arch. The other two stood at attention, one on either side of me, and we waited. One of them barked at me when I tried to look around and ordered me to face forward. To control my increasing anxiety, I took mental notes of these fascinating surroundings and planned a series of paintings in my head, perhaps a medieval-style triptych, oil on old board would work well. The ever-changing interplay of light and shadow cast by the flickering torches would be a challenge to capture. But I felt sure I could come up with something given enough time to experiment with the oils, perhaps a dab here, a smear there of acrylic would do the job. Then there was the pulsating menace radiating off every surface of the chamber I would need to infuse into the painting.

I stuck my hand into the pocket of my trousers and felt my stomach drop as my fingers touched only the lining and a few random pieces of lint. I stuck my hand in the other pocket on the unlikely chance I'd transferred the feather to it or had made a mistake.

'Looking for this?' Leo stepped onto the platform twirling the feather in his hand. He walked to the middle of the platform opposite me, a mocking half-smile on his face, and held it up. He was wearing dark linen trousers and a red Polo shirt. Carino was standing to the side of the platform watching Leo. Blue jeans, white T-shirt, hair slicked back into a short ponytail.

'Feel free to stick that up your ass,' I said. 'Or maybe he can do it for you.' I nodded at Carino, who glanced at me and looked back at Leo.

One of the Polo guys cracked me hard across my face, knocking me off balance into the guy standing on the other side. He pushed me away, and I fell forward on my knees. Leo snapped his fingers, and my escort came out from behind the proscenium arch and waved the others back. Then he stood behind me and pulled me straight up by my arms, pressing his lips to my ear.

'Don't be an idiot. Just answer his questions,' he whispered.

'Take off his cap,' Leo said.

'Let me keep it, please.'

I reached up to hold on to it. But my escort snatched it off my head before I could get to it and tossed it into the shadows.

'Now the shirt,' Leo said.

My escort came around front and ripped open my shirt in one violent tug sending the buttons flying, then yanked it off and let it drop from his fingers.

Leo came down from the platform and touched a finger to my bare chest.

'I always wanted to see this tattoo. I've heard so much about it.' He dragged his finger down from my chest to my stomach, pausing just below my navel.

'All you had to do was ask.'

'Oh, yes?'

I looked him in the eye. 'What am I doing here, Leo?'

Leo nodded then stepped back and leaned against the platform.

'You were warned multiple times to keep away from Beatrice Schein. Mr. Schein warned you, I warned you, Anne Levine warned you, even your tranny girlfriend warned you. And what did you go and do? You got together with Beatrice Schein. Now it's time to pay.'

'I didn't get together with her.'

'We heard different.'

'Then you heard wrong. Beatrice and I are friends. She was having an emotional crisis and came to see me—'

'In your hotel room.'

'Yes, in my goddamn hotel room. She asked to stay the night because she didn't want to be alone, and I slept on the sofa. End of story.'

'You can tell that to Schein when he gets here. In the meantime, we're going to have ourselves a little fun while we wait for him.'

'Be careful, Leo.'

Leo crossed his arms. 'Take off the rest of your clothes.'

'No.'

He nodded at my escort, who punched me in the face so hard I felt like he'd dislocated my jaw. I shook my head against the pain, and everything went black for a moment. I could taste blood in my mouth. My escort grabbed my arm and held me up.

'Let's try that again,' Leo said. 'Take off the rest of your clothes. Unless you prefer for Hugo there to do it for you.'

'You're going to regret this, Leo,' I said. 'All of it.'

Hugo pulled back his arm, ready to smash his fist into my face again, but Leo shook his head.

'I don't believe in regret, my friend. I believe in power. And at the moment, I have it all, and you have none. Now strip off those trousers, or I'll have Hugo there tear them off.'

I glanced at Hugo, then at Carino, then at Leo. They were all staring at me, waiting for me to comply. I looked over my shoulders at the two Polo-shirted guys. They were staring at me too. For a moment I felt time had stopped.

I looked up at the ceiling and noticed for the first time that it was rib-vaulted like in a Gothic church. The dancing red light of the torches cast shifting shadows into the barrels, making it challenging to work out the details. I became suddenly aware of my breathing, more panting than breathing. Loud, raspy, asthmatic. The room felt like it was tipping up on one side. I shifted my weight to avoid falling over. There was movement up there in the shadowy vaulting, almost perpendicular to the platform. I screwed up my eyes to make out what it was. Simmering blackness, a bubble here, a bubble there, breaking the surface, increasing in intensity until the area was seething. Breathe deep, I heard in my head. Slow, deep breaths. *Ten times in; ten times out.* There were birds in the vaulting, scores of them, fluttering madly in the shadows, the sound of their flapping wings filling the chamber. And there among them, I saw Changó. Eyes widened, nostrils flaring, an ax in his hand, ready to strike. *Ten times in; ten times out.*

I looked at Leo again; he was still waiting. Hugo's arm was still pulled back. Carino was no longer there.

I staggered backward, away from Leo, and felt myself come unstuck from myself. It took a moment to realize there were two of me: the Virgilio moving away and the Virgilio that remained standing in front of Leo, his face raised up to the ceiling. I'd shifted to where I could no longer see the vaulted area above the platform, but I could still hear the flapping of the wings. The sound migrated out from under the proscenium, passed overhead, and echoed toward the stairs leading out of the chamber. The next thing I knew I was moving through the side tunnel, racing past Leo's office. I burst into the empty central tunnel and ran the length of it, past the slave stables, past Molly's, footsteps echoing off concrete, *ten times in; ten times out*; past the side tunnels that on all other nights were flaming furnaces of vice consuming the souls of hundreds of men, and that now were yawning sepulchres.

Up ahead, men were dropping into the central tunnel from the access ladder, four of them. Two in dark suits, no tie; Schein's driver; and

Schein himself, immaculately dressed as ever in a grey Armani suit, pink shirt, dark blue tie dotted with pink hand-painted spades. I sped past them as they marched in the direction from where I'd come, and scrambled up the ladder, running past the two men standing guard at the entrance, and bursting out the access door onto the sidewalk outside, finally above ground and drawing in deep draughts of the fresh night air. Schein's limousine was parked next to the van that brought me. There were another couple of cars I didn't recognize. I felt their hoods. They were still warm.

My mother was waiting for me when I arrived at our apartment. She was sitting at the kitchen table taking a sip from a tiny cup of syrup-thick Cuban coffee. She looked up at me as I sat opposite her and shook her head. I took her hand and kissed it. She ran her fingers through my damp hair, then reached over to one side of the table and brought up a flat, white cap, which she put on my head.

'You should never have allowed them to uncover you,' she said. 'You lost power; it weakened you.'

I reached up and felt the cap. 'I didn't have a choice, Mamá.'

'You always have a choice. You could have fought harder to keep it.'

'They would have killed me.'

'They're killing you anyway.'

I looked down at my hands. They were trembling. My mother kissed me on the forehead, lifted my head by my chin and stared into my eyes.

'There's power inside you, hijo. Never doubt that. It's aché. It's right here.' She touched her finger to my forehead. 'I had you sealed when you were a baby. I've been protecting you ever since. But now it's time to protect yourself.'

'I don't deserve any of that, Mamá.' I pointed in the direction of the tunnels. 'I didn't do anything wrong. I've only ever helped people. My whole life...'

'I warned you to stay away from those people, mijo. Even from sweet

Beatrice, who I've come to love as if I'd borne her myself. I knew your association with her would one day lead to this.'

She rose from the table, lit a cigar, and puffed it to life. Then she pointed it at the center of the room.

'Stand there, hijo. One last time.'

She blew smoke all over my body, concentrating most of it where the sacred heart was inked onto my chest, and chanted a prayer in Lucumí. I closed my eyes and drew in the aromatic smoke, filling my lungs with it, exhaling it, once, twice. My mother took me by the hand and led me into my bedroom, out the window, and onto the fire escape. She pointed at the parking lot on the other side of 6th Street. There was only one car parked there. It was Beatrice's Porsche. My heart leaped into my mouth as I lifted my eyes and saw her exiting the far end of the parking lot, running in the direction of the tunnels, accompanied by Marcel. They were following someone who looked like Sexto.

'This is not a punishment, hijo.' My mother took another puff on her cigar and blew a cloud of smoke in their direction. She turned to me. 'This is a test.'

I suddenly found myself back in the underground chamber staring down from the chain-link fence at Schein and Leo, who were standing on the platform staring up at me. My arms were stretched to the sides and affixed to the links with rough twine. There was another length of twine tied around my waist and another around my ankles. I'd been stripped naked, and my face felt swollen and achy. I felt the inside of my mouth with my tongue and found raggedy tender spots and rough edges on a couple of teeth that weren't there before. Schein's stooges were standing off to one side behind the proscenium, murmuring among themselves, disinterested in what was happening in the other part of the room. Schein's driver was leaning against a wall, smoking a cigarette and having a private laugh with himself. I heard Schein saying something about a *tableau vivant*.

'Ironic that the artist should become the painting under these circumstances,' Leo responded.

'Not that I approve of these things, mind you.' Schein nodded at me, speaking to Leo as if I weren't in the room. 'We'll have to discuss this another time. But in this case, it would seem apropos.'

'Mr. Schein...' I croaked, forcing my concentration on him.

'Ah, the subject speaks at last.' Schein crossed his arms and peered at me.

'Let me down.'

He stepped back and extended his arm in an exaggerated flourish. 'Come down from there yourself. You fancy yourself a savior, don't you? Act like one.'

'I didn't sleep with Beatrice,' I said.

'So you've said. But whether you did or whether you didn't, the appearance of evil is often more offensive than the evil itself. Hence, the punishment is deserved.' He glanced at his watch. 'In any case, I'll have these boys cut you down soon; then I never want to see you or hear of you ever again. Your career as an artist is over. We'll be returning this place to its owners, and you will withdraw into your cockroach-infested armpit of a neighborhood, where you can go on playing the voodoo savior to the shopping cart-pushing vermin that infest it, until we tear it all down.'

I could hear the echo of footsteps approaching in the distance. Keen to distract Schein, I jerked my head up and peered into the vaulted area of the ceiling. As I'd hoped, Schein glanced up to see what I was looking at, and the others, noticing the sudden lull in the discussion, did the same. I could just make out the movement I'd seen earlier and heard the sound of fluttering wings. I squeezed my eyes shut and focused on the swirl of phosphenes on the back of my eyelids that became brighter and brighter, a whirlpool of light I willed from my eyes into my head. When I opened them, I saw blackbirds, scores of them, dive bombing

Schein and the others, who slapped them away and ducked for cover.

'Daddy,' Beatrice's voice echoed from the entrance to the chamber.

Schein and Leo whirled around and watched Beatrice and the others run the length of the chamber toward them. Schein's and Leo's stooges streamed out from behind the proscenium and stood in formation in front of the platform, three on each side, while doing their best to avoid the birds that continued to swoop down at them. Schein's eyes went wide when he caught sight of Marcel, who was trailing behind Beatrice. He came down from the platform just as Beatrice reached the front of the chamber. Sexto sprinted past them, leaped onto the platform and reached up to me. He was crying. Leo jumped forward and tried to pull him away. Sexto turned and shoved him hard, sending him tumbling off the platform.

'Take him down,' Sexto screamed.

'Daddy, what are you doing?' Beatrice's face was a cauldron of anxiety as she alternated between looking at her father and monitoring the drama taking place on the platform.

Schein was staring at Marcel slack-jawed, looking less and less like a man in control. The stooges stepped forward, intent on intervening, but were kept back by the birds that continued to swoop at them, cawing and pecking at their heads.

'Stop this now, Daddy!' Beatrice screamed. 'Virgilio didn't do anything.'

Schein pointed at Marcel. 'It's impossible,' he whispered.

Leo scrambled up and snapped his fingers at the stooges, indicating Sexto, who was trying to untie my ankles. As they ascended the stage, Sexto pulled a gun from the waistband of his trousers and pointed it at Leo.

'Tell them to back off, you motherfucker.' Sexto's hand shook as he thrust the gun at Leo.

Everyone in the room turned to look at Sexto.

'Sexto, no,' I screamed. 'Don't do it. They're going to let me down.'

'He deserves it, mano.' Sexto advanced on Leo, his hand steadier now. The tears flowed freely down his face. 'The things he did... I'm going to kill this bastard.'

Leo dove for cover just as Sexto stretched out his arm and fired a shot, hitting him right below his shoulder. Leo cried out and rolled into a corner to the side of the platform behind the proscenium out of sight of the others. The stooges rushed toward Sexto. Carino was now among them; he was wielding a machete. His bared teeth were shining white in the firelight, giving him the same bloodhungry look he had the first time I'd laid eyes on him. Sexto leaped off the platform after Leo before they could reach him. From where I was hanging, I could see the back of his head and shoulders as he stood over Leo.

'Stop, Sexto,' I screamed. 'It's finished.'

An instant later, the sound of three rapid-fire gunshots ricocheted off the walls as Sexto finished off Leo. Carino and the stooges jumped off the stage and rushed Sexto. Two of the Polo-shirted ones disarmed him, hauled him in front of the platform, and dropped him at Schein's feet. Horrified, Beatrice and Schein fell back a few steps to make room for Sexto, who was hyperventilating and rolled into a fetal position. An animal roar filled the chamber, and Carino came bursting out from behind the proscenium, the machete held high. He fell on Sexto and hacked at him, screaming obscenities, and sending blood, bone, and brains flying everywhere. I heard another gunshot ring out; then everything went black.

23

Ad Infero

The first thing I became groggily aware of was pain. Throbbing pain. In my head, my shoulders, my torso, but mainly in my hands. I wanted to feel afraid, but all I was able to muster was a detached sense that my life force was ebbing away. This was compounded by the dull realization that I had no idea where I was; the only clue that I was anywhere was the pain, the intense pain that wracked my body. I had no concept of time passing. Just an ever-present sensation of suffering that could have lasted for an eternity. The hell that everyone talks about. That was it, I realized. I was dead. And paying for my sins.

Then came the moment the pain began to trickle downward, into a sheathe of freezing-heat that started at my toes and slowly worked its way up my legs, my groin, my belly, chest, shoulders and head, as if I were being packed in a container of dry ice. It was the cold of Pluto, a white-hot gelidity that dulled my suffering and slowly, slowly, sent me floating downward into dark oblivion.

Then...

Sounds. Voices. All mixed up. Just at the edge of my consciousness. A maelstrom of beeps, and ring tones, unintelligible phrasings, a Babel of languages, both human and machine. A familiar word. My name perhaps? What was my name? Who was I? I couldn't recall. Not yet.

There it was again. The sharp pain in my hands, followed by a scream. It was *my* scream. I was alive after all. This epiphany flashed across my consciousness as it teetered on the edge of a precipice just moments before it lost its footing and fell again, plunging backwards into the depths of the abyss. *Descensus Christi ad Inferos.*

After what seemed like forever, I surfaced from dark oblivion into bleary awareness, a short, unescorted furlough from God's prison. The blur resolved into a woman's face hovering over me, inches away, her scarlet red mouth moving, uttering words I wasn't able to work out, as all five of my senses weren't yet fully online. Then the grayware kicked in, and my brain finished making the connections: I was in a hospital room, wired up to a clutch of machines. And the in-my-face woman was my mother, Santa Celia, *Madre de Aguas*, reciting an incantation in Lucumí. She hadn't yet noticed that I was conscious. I tried to speak but couldn't make my mouth move. She tossed a glance over her shoulder, then leaned in and, with her leathery thumbs, rubbed something oily and fragrant on my forehead before I faded out again.

'Go back,' spoke a sonorous, musical voice that was neither female nor male. The words echoed in the limitless darkness in which my spirit was cocooned. The bonds were falling away; I sensed a glimmer of light far above me at the top of the pit. My legs were coming free, then my arms, which I strained upward toward the light. My lungs were bursting; I needed desperately to breathe. I swam up, up, clawing and kicking, drawing nearer the light as it increased in near-nova brilliance and rushed at me at warp speed until, at last, I exploded to the surface and—

I opened my eyes and found myself staring at the ceiling of my hospital room, at wispy white clouds drifting past my field of vision. When they finally cleared, I pivoted my head and saw Beatrice curled up in a blue leather chair, her eyes closed, her mouth slightly open. She was dressed in white, her hair tied back with a white band. I looked down at myself and saw that both my hands were bound up in gauze. I brought them close to my face to inspect them more closely. Beatrice stirred awake and glanced over at me. Then, rising from her chair, she stepped slowly to my bedside and tentatively reached out a hand in my direction.

'Virgilio?'

I nodded and smiled weakly.

Beatrice closed her eyes and wrapped her arms around herself, drawing in a deep breath. Tears streamed down her face when she opened them, and she touched my shoulder.

'Oh, Virgilio. Thank God ...'

I tried to speak, but all that came out was a dry croak.

Beatrice shook her head. 'Don't... I've got to alert the doctors. We'll talk after.' She paused at the door for a moment, looked back at me and said in a low voice: 'A lot has happened while you were away.' Then she was gone.

I spent the rest of the afternoon under the care of the medical team, with Beatrice, and later my mother, hovering in the background. According to the doctors, I was expected to make a full recovery, except for my hands, which were beyond repair. Apparently, in the time I was out of body, Leo and his stooges had taken a sledgehammer to them before stringing me up to make sure I never painted again. It would take years of surgeries and rehabilitation before I would be able to use them as anything more than rudimentary paws. At least I was alive...

Once the medical team had finished, a thirtysomething female police detective with a salt-and-pepper bowl cut pushed her way into the room and tried to take a statement from me as part of her investigation into Sexto's murder. I'd been forcefully supressing the memory of that horrible event, waiting until I had the emotional scope to deal with the fallout, along with everything else that had happened. Her questions brought it all back, drowning me in a tidal wave of grief over the loss of my friend, and igniting a fusion of anger at Schein and his people who had set it all in motion. Unable to answer her questions, I jerked my face away and set my jaw, tears streaming out of my eyes. At that, Beatrice leapt forward.

'Why don't you come back another time?' she said with a polite edge in her voice. 'You can see he's upset and exhausted.'

'It's best to take a witness statement when the events are still fresh,' the detective answered firmly.

I shifted back my head and stared at the detective. 'Am I a suspect?'

'Certainly not.'

'Am I under arrest?'

'No.'

'Then, for Christ's sake, please leave your card, and I'll call you when I'm ready to give a statement. I'm not ready yet.'

My mother joined us bedside and nodded at the detective, who had still not left. 'You heard the boy. He'll call you.'

Seeing she was outnumbered, the detective lifted her shoulders and flipped closed her notepad. 'Fine,' she said. 'In any case, we plan on releasing the victim's body to his next of kin before the end of the week.'

'His next of kin is in her eighties and has dementia,' I said, feeling a spike in my blood pressure.

Beatrice touched my arm. 'Leave it with me,' she said, and walked out of the room with the detective, leaving me alone with my mother who stared at me with a mix of tenderness and sadness in her eyes. After a moment of painful silence, I ventured:

'I'm so sorry, Mamá. For everything. I should have listened to you...'

She passed her broad hand over my forehead, pushing back a lock of hair that had fallen over my eye. 'Yes, you should have.' She planted a kiss on my forehead then raised herself to her full height, looking suddenly larger than life in the stark hospital room. 'But everything in this life happens for a reason, hijo, and, in the end, it's all for the best.'

Despite her words, the image of Sexto in his final moments flooded my mind, his desperate, impotent attempts to rescue me, his agonized, pain-filled screams as Carino set upon him. Overwhelmed by it all, I broke down. 'It's my fault...what happened to Sexto,' I said between choking sobs.

'What happened to Sexto was meant to happen. His whole life was leading to that moment. It was his destiny. Just as *this* is yours.' She reached out and touched my gauze-wrapped hands.

Her words sent a chill through my body, and I pulled back my hands. 'I don't understand any of it, Mamá. Sexto was an innocent! And what about me? What am I supposed to do now? I'm a painter without hands, for Christ's sake! How is that for the best?'

She stared at me for a few beats, then she drew a deep breath, bent down and whispered into my ear: 'It's life's greatest mystery, hijo. If you *embrace* it, you'll find yourself. If you rage against it, you're lost.' She gently pulled back my hands and kissed them. 'Embrace it.'

A couple of nights later, following my release from the hospital, I was holed up in my room, in bed and under the covers, feeling desperately sorry for myself. Every so often my mother would knock on my door to announce any number of intending visitors: Beatrice; some colleagues from the art center; a performer from La Noche Buena with an update about Concha; Detective Hardass; but I didn't feel up to seeing anyone. Ever. I refused all of them. The only times I got out of bed were to use the bathroom, or to grab a random bite to eat whenever I felt myself at the point of starvation, or to have a quick smoke. Other than that, I was no better than a pill bug, curled up into a tight little ball, staring at my hairy navel and wishing I were dead. The painter with no hands. What a joke.

Tap, tap, tap.

The insistent sound jarred me out of a fitful sleep. I'd been dreaming of my father again, both of us trapped in an endless dialogue of apologies and recriminations. Still groggy, I felt myself dropping off.

Tap, tap, tap.

I threw off the covers and scanned the darkened room, starting at the door, my closet, the Christ-covered wall, the window.

Tap, tap, tap.

Dragging myself off my bed, I wrapped my naked body in a sheet, shuffled to the window, and pulled back the curtain. I jumped back at the sight of Beatrice in a white turban, crouching on the ledge of the fire escape, her index finger poised in the air, ready to tap again on the glass. I quickly recovered myself and pushed open the sash window with my paws. Beatrice crawled into my room, smoothened out her white skirt, then looked up at me with an earnest expression on her face. I backed away from her and bumped into my bed, and she held out a hand, her wrist festooned with multicolored bracelets.

'Virgilio, wait.'

'I don't want to see anyone. Didn't my mother tell you?'

'Yes, but I had to see you. I couldn't just let you—'

'Couldn't let me what? Feel like shit? And how did you make it up the ladder in that get-up anyway?'

Beatrice looked down at herself for a moment, then sank into a side chair and shook her head, tears standing out in her eyes. I climbed back into bed and stared at her from under my blanket.

'Sexto's funeral,' she whispered. 'It's arranged. Day after tomorrow.'

I sat up. 'You did that?'

She nodded absently. 'It took some doing, as I'm not family. But between the social worker, his grandmother, and I, we were able to get the permissions...'

I felt a hollowness in the pit of my stomach at the mention of Sexto's grandmother. 'How is she? Sexto's grandmother?'

Beatrice held my gaze. 'Not very well, to be honest. Sometimes lucid; sometimes not. I'm not really certain whether she even understands everything that has happened. Maybe it's for the best.'

'You're a good person, Beatrice.'

She waved her hand dismissively. 'She asked about you.'

'Who, Sexto's grandmother?'

Beatrice nodded. 'You should go see her soon. They're not going to let her stay in her house alone for much longer.'

I pulled my blanket around myself tighter. 'Yes, okay. I should.'

The room went quiet for a while, and a chill lingered in the air. Beatrice seemed to be waiting for something. There was an elephant occupying the space between us that neither of us seemed to want to acknowledge. We stared at each other in the silence, knowing that one of us would have to broach the subject. I decided to break the stalemate.

'Am I in danger, Beatrice?'

She sat up slowly in the chair, glancing over her shoulder for a moment before responding.

'Everything's stable for now,' she said cryptically. 'The authorities have agreed to leave everything status quo, as long as my father and his associates lie low.'

'And his redevelopment plans for this neighborhood?'

'That's all on permanent hold. More importantly, he's promised me personally that he'll leave you alone as long as you don't stir things up.' She flashed a sad smile.

I raised myself up and sat cross-legged on my bed, letting the blanket fall around my waist. Beatrice blinked at the tattoo on my chest, then quickly recovered herself.

'So the puppet master's pulled the right marionette strings to get out of trouble,' I said.

Beatrice nodded. 'Something like that.'

'And Carino?'

Beatrice's head snapped up. 'Carino's dead, Virgilio.'

My heart jumped at the news, and my eyes went wide.

'I thought you knew that,' she said.

'Nobody told me.

'Someone shot him just as he was attacking Sexto.'

'Who shot him?'

Beatrice raised her shoulders. 'They're not saying. It could have been the police, or one of my father's men.'

'So that's it then?'

'Yes, that's it.'

Beatrice rose from the chair and sat next to me on the bed. She drew back the covers and exposed my gauze-covered paws, which I raised for her to see.

'Meet the painter without hands.'

She gently pulled them to herself and kissed them, then moved them back onto my lap. 'I have faith you'll recover, Virgilio. You have a great spirit. You care for people. And when you get out of this slump, you'll go on to do great things, whether with your painting or some other way. I sincerely believe that.'

Beatrice's encouragement was exactly what I needed. After she left, I determined to stop feeling sorry for myself, to make an effort to rejoin the world as best I could, and to face the painful realities I'd been avoiding — eyeball to eyeball.

I struggled into a pair of loose-fitting grey sweat pants, a black T-shirt, and a pair of white Vans, and wandered into our living room. My mother had left a plate of rice and black beans for me on the dining table before going to work. Next to the placemat was an unopened letter addressed to me with a French postmark on it and no return address. It reeked of *Obsession*, Concha's favorite perfume. Pinching it between my paws, I pulled it toward my face, and, blinking away the stinging in my eyes, tore open the envelope with my teeth and shook out a single sheet of onionskin. I unfolded it and did my best to decipher Concha's sloppy calligraphy:

Dear Virgilio,

Im fine – in case you were wondering. I've decided to stay in Paris for a while. Im performing in a couple of nightclubs in the Marais, where they LOVE me. And whenever I need money I turn tricks in the Bois du Boulogne. French Men really know how to treat a lady. Anyway...

Enjoy your life Loverboy.

Concha xxx

PS., Fuck you!

I stared at the letter for a bit, then reread it a few more times before folding it closed and working it back into the envelope. I felt terrible for how things had ended between Concha and me and hoped that one day we'd be able to reconcile. But that would have to wait. Right now, I had a friend to bury and a life to rebuild. And an oracle to consult.

An hour later, I was sitting on the ledge of my bridge, my legs dangling over the precipice of the Los Angeles River. It had taken a lot of painful maneuvering with my bound-up hands to make it over the concrete barrier, down the iron ladder and onto the ledge. I still don't know how I managed it that first time. But I did, and was happy to once again be resting my face against the warm vibration of one of its spans. After a few moments of solace, I decided to engage my old friend.

'You're safe now,' I whispered, 'They've cancelled the development plans.'

'Well done,' the bridge answered after a moment. 'But at what cost?'

I held up my hands and, seeing them, felt sad again. 'I'll never paint again, or at least not for a long time. But I saved you, just like I promised.'

'Thank you, my son,' the bridge said. 'The Universe will repay you.'

I stared out over the riverbed in the direction of Long Beach. The sky was starting to lighten with the advancing dawn. 'Maybe it will; maybe it won't.' I pulled myself up to my feet. 'Anyway, it doesn't matter. It is what it is, and I have to just get on with things.'

'What will you do?'

The question hung in the air unanswered, and I readied myself to go.

'What will you do?'

A truck rumbled overhead on its way over the bridge to the central delivery depot, followed by a couple of random cars. I glanced up and watched as they receded into the distance.

'What will you do?'

I kissed the span and shuffled toward the iron ladder, preparing to make the challenging climb up to the street. Rosa's on 4th Street would be opening soon. I'd grab a cup of coffee and a pastry there and then head over to see Sexto's grandmother first thing.

'What will you do?'

Finally, standing at street level after considerable effort, I mopped my brow with the back of my forearm and looked up and down 6th Street with its cracked sidewalks, industrial buildings, and crumbling tenements. Soon it would be choked with traffic. But now, at this time, it was still peaceful. The sight of it warmed me and brought a smile to my lips.

'What will—'

I held up my hand at the bridge and shook my head. 'Leave that with me.'

And with that, I turned my back on the bridge and headed up Santa Fe Street toward Rosa's. I had my whole life in front of me, with years enough to figure things out. Right now, though, it was time for coffee.

24

Pinnacle

The last time I saw Beatrice was graveside following Sexto's poorly attended funeral. The sun was at its zenith in the cloudless sky and mercilessly pounded down on those few of us who had accompanied his casket from the chapel to his final resting place. Beatrice was radiant in a white headscarf, flowing white dress, white gloves, and white pumps, shining like an angel in the reflected sunlight. Marcel was standing next to her in a black suit, dark sunglasses obscuring his eyes.

My mother poked her head out of the chapel and surveyed the cemetery, shielding her eyes against the sun with her broad palm. When she spotted us, she stepped out and navigated the long gravel path snaking toward us, puffing on a fat cigar. She hobbled forward with the aid of a walking stick, bearing an unseen weight on her back and shoulders. The priest waited for her to arrive, then uttered a final prayer over the grave and stepped back as the cemetery workers swooped in to shovel dirt into it.

My mother rested her walking stick against a tree, then took Beatrice and me by the hand and walked us a little distance from Sexto's grave to a small stand of junipers, leaving Marcel to head back to the chapel alone.

She blew a protective cloud of smoke over each of us and drew us close, chanting something in Lucumí I didn't recognize before withdrawing and leaving us alone.

Beatrice and I stared at each other for a few minutes, holding hands, neither of us saying a word. Her lovely eyes transmitted that mix of confidence, worldliness, vulnerability, and innocence I had come to love, and I felt suddenly moved to the very depths of my soul at the thought I wouldn't be seeing her again for a long while. Beatrice removed her gloves and wiped away the tears that were coursing down my face, then kissed me on the cheek and smiled, her eyes shining in the bright sunlight.

'Sweet Savior,' she said. 'Don't be sad.'

I started to laugh, but then felt a tide of sadness well up inside of me again. I dropped to one knee and choked back the sobs. Beatrice put her hand on my back and kept it there until I regained control. Then we hugged, and I made her promise to stay in contact wherever she went in the world.

And then she was gone.

She had entered my world as if descending from Heaven, intent on pulling me out of Hades, only to be pulled into it herself. Only, there was no Heaven; and Hades had proven to be the doorway through which she passed on her journey to a new world and, phoenix-like, to that supernova of self-discovery, her soul ascending into the African sky out of twisted metal and flaming wreckage.

I wandered up the hill through the gravestones until I was standing at the highest point of the cemetery overlooking Downtown LA, shimmering like a mirage through a dingy layer of smog in the intense heat. I removed my shirt, mopped my face with it, and raised my ruined hands to the sky, in a gesture of blessing, an embrace, an act of defiance. I was a painter with no hands. So be it. After all that had passed, I wanted badly to believe that it was all part of a master plan. Destiny was real, and mine was somewhere out there, spread out before me at my feet. I was Christ standing on the pinnacle of the Temple. There was no Satan at my side. I was ready to leap.

A Note on Santería

When hundreds of thousands of members of the Yoruba people were brought as slaves from eastern Africa to Cuba in the nineteenth-century, their traditional African religion absorbed significant elements of Roman Catholicism. The resulting syncretion, or fusion, is called Santería, "the way of the saints." The Cuban Yoruba express their devotion to spirits, called *orishas*, through the iconography of Catholic saints. Catholic symbols are often present at Santería rites, and Santería devotees attend the Catholic sacraments.

Santería teaches that each and every individual has a destiny from God. This destiny is fulfilled with the aid and energy of the orishas, which each devotee seeks by nurturing a personal relationship with his or her personal orisha. According to the teachings of Santería, whilst the orishas are powerful beings, they are not immortal. Their survival depends on animal sacrifice. Hence, one of the principal forms of devotion in Santería is animal sacrifice.

In Santería, sacrifices are performed at birth, marriage, and death rites, for the cure of the sick, for the initiation of new members and priests, and during an annual celebration. Animals sacrificed in Santería rituals include chickens, pigeons, doves, ducks, guinea pigs, goats, sheep, and turtles. The animals are killed by the cutting of the carotid arteries in the neck. The sacrificed animal is cooked and eaten, except after healing and death rituals.

Santería adherents faced widespread persecution in Cuba, so the religion and its rituals were practiced in secret, behind the veil of

Catholicism. To this day, the open, unsyncretised practice of Santería and its rites is rare and infrequent. The religion was brought to the United States primarily by exiles from the Cuban revolution. The number of practitioners in the United States alone is estimated at somewhere between 20,000 to 50,000.

[*Source*. Church of the Lukumi Babalu Aye, Inc. c. Hialeah, 508 U.S. 520 (1993)]

About the Author

Orlando Ortega-Medina studied English Literature at UCLA and has a law degree from Southwestern University School of Law in Los Angeles. At university, he won The National Society of Arts and Letters award for Short Stories. In 2017, his collection Jerusalem Ablaze: Stories of Love and Other Obsessions was shortlisted for the UK's Polari First Book Prize, and in 2018 he was named the Marilyn Hassid Emerging Author for the Houston Jewish Book and Arts Festival. Ortega-Medina lives in London.